D1363290

OTHER BOOKS IN THE SERIES

Starring Sammie . . . as the girl who becomes a big
fat liar (but whose pants *don't* catch fire)

Starring Brody . . . as the model from the States
(who's in a bit of a state herself)

Starring Alex . . . as the girl with the voice
of an angel (who can be a little
devil too)

Starring Jolene . . .

. . . as the runaway who's trying to do a good turn
(just make sure she doesn't turn on you)

Helena Pielichaty
Illustrated by Melanie Williamson

OXFORD
UNIVERSITY PRESS

OXFORD
UNIVERSITY PRESS

Great Clarendon Street, Oxford OX2 6DP

Oxford University Press is a department of the University of Oxford.
It furthers the University's objective of excellence in research, scholarship,
and education by publishing worldwide in

Oxford New York

Auckland Bangkok Buenos Aires Cape Town
Chennai Dar es Salaam Delhi Hong Kong Istanbul Karachi
Kolkata Kuala Lumpur Madrid Melbourne Mexico City Mumbai
Nairobi São Paulo Shanghai Taipei Tokyo Toronto

Oxford is a registered trade mark of Oxford University Press
in the UK and in certain other countries

British Library Cataloguing in Publication Data available

ISBN 0-19-275250-2

1 3 5 7 9 10 8 6 4 2

Designed and typeset by Mike Brain Graphic Design Limited, Oxford

Printed in Great Britain by
Cox & Wyman Ltd, Reading, Berkshire

for
my youngest niece
Mathilda May Pielichaty
with love

with grateful thanks to:
Graham, Rita, Karen, and Fiona

Welcome to
ZAPS

Contact: Jan Fryston NNEB (Supervisor)

on 07734-090876 for details.

Please note: Mr Sharkey, headmaster of Zetland Avenue Primary School, politely requests parents/carers <u>not</u> to contact the school directly as the After School Club is independent of the school and he wants it to stay that way!

All children must be registered before they attend.

Zetland Avenue Primary School (ZAPS) After School Club

Newsletter

Dear Parents and Carers,

We have lots of exciting things planned for this year and hope you will tell your friends and neighbours all about us. Children do not have to attend Zetland Avenue Primary School to come to After School Club; any child is welcome as long as they are aged between five and eleven and have been registered.

Special Events:

1. November: **Children in Need Fundraising.** We will be joining in with the main school's activities. We wonder what Mr Sharkey will be getting up to this year? (If you remember, last year he sat in a bath of smelly jelly!)

2. February half-term holiday: **Film-making Week.** Media Studies students from Bretton Hill College will be showing us how to make and star in a real film. Watch out, Hollywood!

3. Easter: **Pop Kids.** We will be staging a talent show to perform in front of parents and carers.

4. Summer: **Get Active!** Summer Sports activities for everyone throughout the holidays.

Also: E-PALS

Once the new computers have been installed we are hoping to set up an Internet connection to After School Clubs throughout the UK. Children who are interested will be able to write to their 'E-pals' from Penzance to Pitlochry!

See you all soon,

Jan

Jan Fryston (Supervisor)

After School Club

Sammie Wesley

Reggie Glazzard

Alex McCormack

Lloyd Fountain

Mrs Fryston
Supervisor

Mrs McCormack
Assistant

Brody Miller

Sam Riley

Jolene Nevin·

Brandon Petty

Some comments from our customers at the After School Club:

'It's better than going round my gran's and having to watch Kung Fu films all day in the holidays'—

Brandon Petty, Y1

'It's good because I am home-schooled so the After School Club gives me a chance to mix with children my own age and make new friends.'

Lloyd Fountain, aged 9

'I love going to ZAPS After School Club— there's so much to do. It's a blast.'

(Brody Miller, Y6)

— You feel at ease
— On the purple settees
— The staff are kind
— And help you unwind
— So come along
— You can't go wrong

— (Sam Riley, Y5)

'After School Club is OK, apart from the rats and poisonous biscuits.' (Don't worry folks – just messing with your minds – Ha! Ha!)

Reggie G. aged 133*

*our resident comedian informs me he prefers to use months to describe his age – JF

'There's not nowhere better than After School Club and I like Mrs Fryston because she is kind and understands how you feel about things.'

Sammie Wesley Y5

'I've been to other After School Clubs before but they've been rubbish and I've always been kicked out but this one is the best.'

Jolene Nevin Y5

'I have been coming to After School Club since it started because my mum is one of the helpers. I enjoy the craft activities and when new people start, like Jolene.'

Alex McCormack Y4

What do you think? Add your own comment

Chapter One

Before I start, if you're one of those people who think boys are 'cool' and kittens are 'sweet' and you have hundreds of lip glosses in different flavours like raspberry ripple and pina colada, I don't think you should read my story. You won't like it—it'll be too real for you.

My anger-management counsellor would tell me off for putting that and say something like, 'Aren't you being a little judgemental, Jolene? A bit alienating?' And then I'd have to say: 'Again in English, please, miss?' and she'd remember I'm only just ten and put it into simple words like: 'Some people can like kittens and wear lip gloss and live in the real world, you know.'

And I'd say, 'Yeah, right, name me one.'

I think my counsellor might be quite new to the business. She keeps coming up with real no-brainers. Today, for instance, Friday, she told me to make a list of targets for over the summer holidays, which begin on Monday. 'Six weeks is a long time for you at home without the structure of school, Jolene, and I know you sometimes find a change of routine a challenge.'

'What do you mean?' I asked her.

'Well, if we look at some episodes from your past, changes seem to have been a trigger for some of your worst . . . erm . . . incidents. When your mum got married to Darryl, for instance?'

'What about it?'

'Didn't you run away from school several times?'

'I didn't run away. I just went visiting Spencer in Newcastle. I was worried about him,' I told her.

'Spencer?'

'Mam's old boyfriend. He works at the station in the baguette bar. She chucked him for Darryl and he was gutted.'

'But Newcastle is miles away from Washington. It was a dangerous thing to do.'

'It is when you're wearing a Sunderland shirt,' I said which I thought was funny but she didn't get it and I couldn't be bothered to explain football rivalry to her.

'Then there was the time you were sent to stay at your grandad Jake's house in Yorkshire and you attended an after-school club with your Auntie Brody,' she continued. 'Didn't you end up in some sort of trouble there? By all accounts you were pretty unmanageable when you returned.'

Flaming hot-pants, I thought, trying to peer over the top of her folder. Did she have what I'd had for breakfast written down there and all? I stared at my feet and said I didn't remember, though of course I did.

Between you and me, what happened at Brody's—she's only eleven so there's no way I'm calling her 'auntie'—wasn't one of my best childhood moments—though it certainly wasn't my worst by a long chalk—but all the same I didn't really appreciate counsellor-lady bringing it up. You'd have thought she'd have better manners.

Counsellor-lady sighed and looked at her watch. I knew the meter was ticking and she had to see loads more bad kids after me. First though, she scribbled something in her folder, then threw me an apologetic smile. 'Just try to stay out of trouble, Jolene, for six weeks. You're such a bright girl, with bags of potential. Put everything I've taught you over the past few sessions into action. Remember, if you feel yourself struggling to keep your temper . . .'

'Yeah, I know, sing a song or repeat a rhyme,' I said. 'Can I go now, please?'

Chapter Two

Straight after my session I headed for the minibus that took me to Burnside After School Club. I can't go to the after-school club at my school because I've been banned, so I am taken across town to another one where I can't put paint in the playleader's coffee or throw chairs through the window. As you have probably guessed, it's little episodes like that which have got me seeing counsellor-lady twice a term in the first place. I'm not bothered though because the club at Burnside's mint and I wouldn't have been sent there if I'd been a goody-goody.

The club's in the dining hall of the old part of Burnside Parochial Juniors. The school itself has been rebuilt in the playing fields across from it and is brand spanking new but they still keep the old bit open for community things like Slimmin' Wimmin and our after-school club.

Mick, the boss-man, is all right. He's a retired Youth Club leader and knows how to handle me. He lays on plenty of physical activities to tire me out at the beginning then lets me spend the rest of the session e-mailing my friend Alex McCormack, who goes to that other after-school club counsellor-lady mentioned. Actually, now I come to think about it, that week at Brody's wasn't all bad—I did get my one true mate out of it.

As usual, there was an e-mail from Alex waiting for me when I got to the club, with an attachment telling me what her club, ZAPS, had got lined up for their summer activities. 'Hey, sir,' I said to Mick after I had written back to her, 'what are we doing special during the holidays? At my mate's after-school club they've got football and a climbin' wall and all sorts. Can we have any of this?'

I stuck the list of activities under his nose to show him. Mick scratched his beard and looked fed up. I've never seen Mick look fed up before. 'I'm sorry, Jolene, pet,' he said, then turned to the whole group and went, 'I'm sorry, all of you. I've got some bad news . . .' Then he told us the council had found something called asbestos in the old ceilings and outbuildings and it meant they had to close down the after-school club until they'd got rid of it. 'So there won't be anything on here until September,' he said sorrowfully, 'which is ridiculously short notice, I know.'

What was it counsellor-lady said about me not reacting well to sudden changes of routine? Huh, it was Mam she should have been worried about, not me. To say she took the news badly is putting it mildly. Ballistic is more like it—I thought she was going to crash the car. 'What?' she said, trying to straighten the steering wheel, all her silver bracelets jangling at once along her arms, 'this had better not be a wind up, Jolene, or I'll kill you.'

'Looks like you're going to anyway,' I pointed out.

She glared at me through the rear-view mirror and told me to stop being so clever.

'You were going a bit fast, Claire,' Keith said in his tiny-tinny eight-year-old voice from the front. He's Darryl's eldest. There's him and his brother Jack. Jack's six. They're both wet and whingy and they hate football and never swear. We've got nothing in common.

Mam apologized for speeding immediately and slowed right down for the little slug. 'Was I, pet? I'm sorry, it's just I'd made some plans and Jolene's news came as a bit of a shock.'

'What plans?' I asked, immediately suspicious. She was always doing this—coming up with 'plans'. Mam's plans usually ended up with her going off somewhere without me. I'm not talking an afternoon shopping at the Metro Centre, neither. She left me at Nana's for four years once.

'Never you mind,' she said, going straight ahead at the roundabout instead of turning left onto our estate.

I pulled a face at the back of her head and Jack giggled until I gave him the daggers. We were heading for Nana's. That was nothing to giggle about.

Chapter Three

'What are we coming here for?' I asked as Mam pulled up outside Nana's front gate. 'Isn't Nana at work?' I was hot and tired and just wanted to go home. Nana's house always made me depressed.

'She's had today off and I've got to sort something out,' Mam said, putting on the handbrake and leaning across to check her lipstick in the mirror. Mam's very precise about her appearance. Her hair is always blonde. Her skin is always tanned and her clothes are always tight-fitting to show off her figure. She never eats bread, rice, pasta, or potatoes and never weighs above eight and a half stone. 'Now, boys,' she said as we followed her up the path, 'I want you just to watch telly for five minutes while I talk to Nana Lynne. You, too, Jolene. I've got to ask Nana a big favour and I don't want any interruptions.'

'What favour?' I demanded.

'That's for me to know and you to find out!' Mam said lightly.

Despite the heat of the afternoon, my hands felt cold and clammy. She was up to something. I could feel it.

Nana took ages to answer the door and I half hoped she had gone out. Eventually we heard the pat-pat-pat of her espadrilles and there she stood. Like Mam, Nana was always blonde, always tanned, and always wore tight clothes, though unlike Mam she had a scraggy neck and veins running down the backs of her legs like blue worms. 'Oh, it's you,' she said, tying a knot in her sarong over her bony hips, 'I was sunbathing round the back.' Her face was pink and flushed but I knew from the way she swayed in the doorway her high colour had nothing to do with the sun. 'Come on in,' she trilled, beckoning us through. 'Isn't it gorgeous weather? I bet you've been roasted in that salon,' Nana said to Mam.

'Tell me about it,' Mam replied, undoing the top buttons of the white receptionist's uniform she wears to Pluckin' Mel's Beauty Emporium.

In the kitchen, Nana refilled her wine glass with a dark red drink from a jug in the fridge. 'Help yourselves to Coke, kids—but don't touch this, will you?' she said. 'That's Lynne's special pop!' And she laughed so hard her boobs shook. Jack and Keith looked at each other, not knowing what to say. I wrinkled my nose at her in disgust.

'Where's Martin?' Mam asked, fetching three glasses down from the shelf and filling them with cola.

Martin was Nan's second husband, Mam's stepdad. He's a security guard in a builder's yard which suits him because he's a plank. 'Martin?' Nana frowned as if she couldn't remember who he was. 'Oh, he'll be back soon—he's just been out to buy some stuff for his pack-up. He's on nights this week.'

I was glad he was out and I hoped whatever Mam had to say would be quick so I didn't have to see him.

We didn't exactly get on, Grandad Martin and me. You could say we rubbed each other up the wrong way. 'You go sit in the front room now while I go talk,' Mam said, ushering us out with the back of her hand. She leaned close to me and whispered in my ear, 'Behave yourself and I'll give you a tenner.' I stared at her in amazement. Resorting to bribery so early in the proceedings? What was she up to?

Nana's front room was dark and stuffy. She never drew the curtains back in summer because she didn't want the sun to fade the furniture, so the three of us sat on her pale blue leather settee and sipped our drinks in the gloom. Outside, I could hear Mam and Nana chatting in the garden but not clearly enough over the noise from the cartoons on TV to hear the actual words.

The cartoon was boring but Jack and Keith sat and wordlessly watched every flicker, just like they'd been told. They were so obedient I reckon they'd been sheepdogs in their last life.

I couldn't stand it any longer and went into the kitchen to try and listen in on what Mam was up to, but just as I reached the back door, I heard the front door open and I quickly pretended to be getting more Coke from the fridge.

'Who's that?' Grandad Martin asked sharply, entering the kitchen and dropping a Spar carrier bag onto the table. He was a small, wiry man with sharp eyes that burned into you. I always felt I'd done something wrong when I was with him.

'It's only me. I was just getting a drink,' I said quickly in case he realized what I was up to.

He dragged out a chair and sat down. 'Pour me one while you're at it, then, Billy No-Mates. Don't take the lot,' he warned, scowling at me. See, he'd started already, teasing me. Billy No-Mates. Huh! Better than Billy No-Brains like him.

'I wasn't taking the lot,' I said, scowling right back and searching for another glass.

'Who else is here then, Billy?' he asked, his sharp eyes flashing towards the back door.

'Mam and Keith and Jack.'

'Thh! Bang goes my bit of peace and quiet before I go to work then.'

Charming. He's not like this with my cousins, by the way. He acts like a proper grandad towards them, all piggy-back rides and day trips out. It's just us he's got a downer on and me in particular. 'We're not stopping long,' I said.

He scratched the back of his shortly-cropped head and sniffed. 'Where've I heard that one before?'

I took a long sip of my drink, my hands shaking as I held the glass. We both knew what he was referring to—the time when I was two and Mam had gone off to work on the cruise ships and hadn't come back until I was six. 'Mam's just popped in to see Nana, that's all. It's what daughters do!' I said defensively.

'Huh! It might be what normal daughters do but Claire's never been normal, has she? And if she's just popped round, how come she phoned earlier to make sure we'd be in?'

He looked searchingly at me as if I had the answer but all I could do was shrug. I hadn't known about the phone call and the news of it did nothing to take away that weird feeling I had in my stomach. 'Just popped in,' Grandad Martin repeated, 'that'll be the day. Where is she?'

'In the garden.'

'Hm.' He drained his glass in one go and stood up, nodding towards the loaf of bread sticking out of the carrier bag. 'While you're here you might as well make yourself useful. I'll have two rounds—ham and mustard,' he said and headed out towards the back garden.

I was tempted to ask him what his last servant had died of but I did as I was told, though I *might* have put a bit too much mustard on the ham. Well, it came out of the jar too fast, didn't it? Mustard does that sometimes, especially the really *hot* variety. That would give the old misery-guts something to think about when he was sitting in his hut tonight, I thought with a grin.

I'd just finished wrapping the sandwiches in cling-film when Grandad Martin returned. 'Gab, gab, gab,' he said, referring to Mam and Nana and flung himself down into the chair right next to me.

'What did Mam say?' I asked, trying not to show how keen I was to know the answer.

He glared at me but didn't reply, though there was something in his eyes I couldn't quite fathom. From the breast pocket on his England T-shirt, he withdrew a rectangular pile of scratch cards which he unfolded and laid flat on the table. I watched as he took his 'lucky' coin from his shorts and began to rub the metallic-grey seals on the top card.

The first two revealed identical cash prizes of ten thousand pounds but the third didn't match up, as usual. You had to get all three to win. Exactly the same happened on the second card on the strip, and the third, and the fourth.

'Hard luck,' I said as his face clouded over.

'Hard luck? Aye, that's all I get is hard luck. Working my socks off for a minimum wage while all that fairy down south does is point a camera and he's a millionaire. Where's the justice?'

Here we go, I thought. 'That fairy down south' was my other grandad, Grandad Jake, Nana's first husband. Grandad Martin is always having a dig at him because Jake is a famous photographer and rolling in it and it annoyed him no end.

'And there's no need for you to pull that face,' Grandad Martin said sourly.

'I wasn't.'

'I know what you're thinking.'

'No you don't.'

I'd be grounded for life if he did.

'You're thinking, "I wish Grandad Martin lived in a flashy house instead of this old dump".'

'Yeah, right,' I mumbled. There was no point even trying to contradict him when he started on like this. What a pair my grandparents were. Nana sozzled one half of the time and Grandad Martin feeling sorry for himself the other half.

Absent-mindedly, he picked up one of the torn scratch cards and began to clean between his teeth with a corner of it. 'You're just the same as your mother. Nothing was ever good enough for her.'

Another familiar line, just because I'm the spitting image of Mam when she was my age. 'Mm,' I said, trying not to look at the soggy segment which, job done, he threw back onto the table. Next, Grandad reached behind him for his Tupperware box and dropped his sandwiches into it, followed by a bag of pork scratchings, muttering that he bet Jake Miller wouldn't be having pork scratchings for his supper. He then fastened the lid of his sandwich box down firmly, running his fingers and thumbs along the edge like a pastry cook finishing a pie. 'But where was *he* when your nana and me were bringing Claire up, eh? Nowhere, Billy No-Mates. Just remember that—

nowhere. Not that you'd know it from the way Claire bangs on about him.'

I began to get irritated. 'Stop calling me Billy No-Mates. It's annoying.'

'It's only the truth.'

'It's not.'

'Isn't it? Name me one friend then,' he retorted, 'cos I've never met one.'

'Easy—Alex McCormack, so there.'

'Never heard of her.'

'That's your problem,' I told him.

'No,' he said grumpily, 'my problem is I've got landed with you and your cheek for two weeks.'

My stomach clenched as his dark eyes met mine. 'What do you mean?' I asked, blinking hard.

'Caught you by surprise, has it? Why? I told you, Claire doesn't "pop in". Not without wanting something. You're staying with us for a fortnight while she goes on holiday—not that we'll get any thanks for it.'

'On holiday?'

'Yes. And bang goes mine.'

Chapter Four

It was true. Mam told me on the way home—a belated honeymoon for her and Darryl, booked on the 'spur of the moment'. Jack and Keith were already taken care of because they were at their mam's for a month so that just left me to worry about. Sure, if she'd known earlier about the after-school club closing, she might have thought twice about booking but the tickets were bought now and I'd be fine because she'd give Nana plenty of money to cover everything.

'Take me with you, Mam, I'll be good, I promise,' I asked her the next day as she packed yet another bright pink bikini into her suitcase.

'Don't start, Jolene,' Mam warned.

'Please? I don't want you to go away without me.'

Mam crossed over to her pine dresser and took out a pile of underwear, not even looking at me. 'Jolene, it's only for two weeks. Aren't I allowed two weeks off from you? What are we? Joined at the hip?' she asked, checking her watch.

'I don't want to stay at Nana's.'

'Well, who else'd have you, with your temper tantrums? I'm amazed she still said yes after I told her about the after-school club shutting.'

'But I don't want to stop with them. They're always arguing and Grandad Martin's a miserable maggot.'

Mam just glared at me. 'Look, if you're sweet to him, he'll be sweet to you.'

'I don't want to be sweet to him!' I protested. 'Being sweet's for girls!'

'Oh, just go away, Jolene—give me five minutes' peace!' Mam snapped.

'Why should I?' I snapped back.

'Because you're getting on my nerves.'

'Ask me if I'm bothered!' I shouted, breathing the hard, shallow breaths that scared me.

Just then Darryl came into the bedroom, holding a foul orange and lime-green Hawaiian shirt over his pot belly. 'What do you think of this little number, eh?' he asked and winked at me.

He was always winking at me. Winking at me and butting in when he wasn't wanted, the daft plonker.

'Oh, Darryl,' Mam laughed, 'I'm not being seen out with you wearing that!'

'Oh, why not? What's wrong with it?' Darryl asked, pretending to be upset. 'What do you think, Jolene? Don't you think I'll knock them Benidorm lasses for six in this?'

'Who cares?' I said, glowering at him. I just wanted him to go away so I could talk to Mam in private, to sort out this whole mess.

Darryl's face fell. 'I was just trying to be friendly, pet,' he said, glancing at Mam as if to say, 'What's up with her now?'.

'Ignore her,' Mam instructed, taking the shirt and swiftly folding it against her chest. 'She's in a strop because we're having some time off together. Being with her fifty weeks of the year isn't good enough for her. She always has to spoil things.'

I stared at my mam, my ears filling with a sharp whooshing sound. Spoil things? What did she expect after a bombshell like this? Applause? A beach towel was thrown on to the bed and I swept it onto the floor. 'You never listen, do you? You're a rubbish mother, you are!' I fumed as the hailstorm passed but sparks circled round my head instead, crashing into each other and making tiny explosions.

'Oh, we're off!' Mam sighed, casually bending to pick up the towel. 'Fat lot of good those anger-management lessons are doing her. I knew they'd be a waste of time.'

I tried to think quickly about which rhyme I'd chosen for counsellor-lady but I didn't have time. All I could think about was the fact that Mam was leaving me again, dumping me without any build up, any warning. What if she was lying? Not going for two weeks at all but three? Four? A year . . .

The sparks were blinding me and I had to let go. Had to let all that anger out. 'All you care about is your stupid holiday!' I screamed, and lunged towards her suitcase, tossing all the neatly piled clothes out, throwing them across the bed, over my shoulder, at her face, every which way I could. 'You don't think about me, being left behind!' A shoe went flying into the table lamp, knocking it sideways with a satisfying clatter. The hairdryer would have been next—that was heading for the mirror—only Darryl seized it and told me to let go.

'Please, love,' he said.

'I'm not your love! I'm not anyone's love,' I shouted, dropping the hairdryer and running out.

Chapter Five

I spent the rest of the day in my room, having pushed my chest of drawers against the door so nobody could come in. Not that anybody tried, which was fine by me. I watched telly and played on my Playstation and read a bit, then went to bed. When I awoke, I felt different. A coldness had taken over my heart. If she didn't care about me, I decided, I didn't care about her. Let her go to Benidorm. Ask me if I'm bothered.

That day, Sunday, was spent seeing Jack and Keith off when their mam arrived. Her name's Tracie and she's a rubbish mother too. I once asked her how come she didn't have Jack and Keith full-time instead of Darryl and she told me to mind my own business. 'It is my business when they've taken over my bedroom,' I told her—among other things involving swear words. I'm not allowed to be around when she arrives now.

Everybody pretended to be pally and civilized as they swapped kids but then Jack got tearful when it was time to say goodbye and he clung to Darryl's neck so hard that in the end he had to prise him off and force him into the car. I could have sworn I saw Darryl brush a tear away from his eye when he came into the house. How sloppy can you get?

There were no tears from me when it was my turn the next morning. There might have been once. Last time Mam did this, dumping me on Grandad Jake miles and miles away, I was as wet as Jack had been, begging her not to leave me. Not this time, though, not even when she began making a big fuss of me before we left the house, hugging me and telling me it would soon pass. I'd had enough. Not that I let her see how I really felt. I was a hundred per cent sugar and spice when we arrived outside Nana's at seven o'clock. I had to be, if my plan was going to work.

I just hopped out of the car and told Mam not to bother getting out. 'Are you sure, darlin'?' she said, leaning out of the passenger window but looking relieved.

I fixed a big, brave smile on my face. 'Sure I'm sure.'

'We're still mates, aren't we?' she asked, stroking my Sunderland shirt sleeve. That was her way of saying she forgave me about the suitcase incident.

'Way-ay, man,' I grinned, stretching the smile as far as it would go.

Mam smiled back. 'You can be so lovely, sometimes, Jolene! And you could be so pretty if only you'd wear something else.' She shook her head and let go of my sleeve, delving into her handbag. 'Here then, take this and give it to Nana—not Grandad Martin, OK? I don't want it all to go on scratch cards.' She handed me a white envelope I knew contained my board and lodging for the fortnight. I knew Grandad Martin wouldn't have agreed to have me without it. 'And if Martin teases you, just ignore him,' she added. Her eyes darted towards Nana's house which, like all the others along the street, still had its curtains drawn. 'Be quiet when you go in—he might just have got in from work.'

'I will be,' I promised. 'Have a great time.'

Darryl then leaned across her and gave me a twenty pound note. 'And you take this for ice creams, pet,' he beamed.

'Thanks,' I shrugged and stuffed it in my pocket. Every little helped.

I opened the gate to Nana's house quietly as Darryl did a three point turn in the road. I walked slowly up the path towards the front door, put one hand towards the doorbell and turned and waved with the other. As soon as the car was out of sight, I legged it to the nearest bus stop.

By seven thirty I was in Washington bus station. By eight thirty I was at Newcastle Central Station having a nice old chinwag with Spencer and by nine o'clock I was on a train to Wakefield with a free tuna and sweetcorn baguette in one hand and an open return ticket in the other. Well, so what? I thought to myself as fields flashed by the window of the White Rose Express. Everyone else is having a holiday, why not me?

Chapter Six

It wasn't until I got off the train at Wakefield I realized I might not have thought my plan through. For example, when you're visiting a mate, it helps if you know their address. I only knew Alex lived near Zetland Avenue Primary School but I didn't know where that was. The bus station was my best bet, but I wasn't sure where that was, either. I'd only been to Wakefield once and then I'd arrived by car in the dark. Still, I hadn't travelled this far to be put off by minor details like that. Hitching my backpack higher over my shoulders, I headed out of the station and towards the town centre.

I had only gone about a hundred metres when I knew I had really screwed up. Alex would think it was mint to see me but what about her mam, Mrs McCormack? Mrs McCormack worked at the After School club and was one of those fussy women who did everything by the book. She'd have a million questions about how I'd arrived all alone and out of the blue. She wouldn't believe anything I told her.

I sighed and glanced across the road. There was a restaurant there—Piccollino's—I remembered it from my last visit. A grin broke across my face. Mrs McCormack wouldn't believe a pack of lies—but I knew a man who would.

I returned to the station and sat on an empty bench on the far side of the platform. There, I dialled Grandad Jake's mobile number from Mam's mobile which I'd pinched from her bag while she was flapping over the packing this morning. He answered instantly. 'Yep, it's Jake.'

'Hi, Grandad Jake, it's me, Jolene.'

'Jolene?' he said, sounding puzzled. Well, he would. I

haven't spoken to the guy in months. We're not what you'd call a close-knit family.

I tried to sound equally puzzled back. 'I was just wondering where you were?'

'What do you mean?'

'Well, I've arrived at the station but you're not here. I wondered if you'd got caught up in traffic or something, like?'

'Hang fire a minute . . .' There was a pause while he shouted at someone in the background. 'Not there—there—by the orange snowman. Jolene? Are you still there? What station?'

'Wakefield, of course.'

'Wakefield? Wakefield Westgate?'

'Yes. Mam did tell you . . . didn't she?' I said slowly, trying to sound calm but with a hint of panic round the edges.

'Tell me what?' he sighed. He knew, you see. He knew from last time that having his ten-year-old granddaughter turn up unexpectedly on his doorstep was not unimaginable—not with a daughter like he'd got.

'That you were looking after me for two weeks while she went on holiday.'

'What?'

'On holiday,' I repeated loudly, 'Benidorm. They should be landing in Alicante any time now. She did tell you? I know she was having trouble getting through to you but she said she'd left messages.'

'For Pete's sake! I knew nothing about it. I'm not even at home, I'm in London . . . No, not on the snowman, next to it, man! And leave those elves alone! Jolene, this isn't a joke, is it?'

'No, Grandad, course not.' As if to prove where I was, a 125 came hurtling through the station, drowning out his next sentence.

'I can't even send you up to the house. Kiersten and Brody have gone to the States already . . .' he repeated.

Result! Kiersten, Grandad's second wife, was American—they always spent summer in America. No interrogation from the missus to follow. No quizzical glances from lip gloss daughter Brody. This got better and better. 'I could always catch a train to London and meet you there,' I began. I fancied a trip to London. Madame Tussaud's was supposed to be dead good. There's this Chamber of Horrors . . .

'No!' Grandad Jake barked. 'I'm not having you travelling on your own.'

'But I've just come from Newcastle by myself . . .'

'Never mind! Claire must be crazy putting you on a train alone. Jeez! She's pulled some fast ones in her time but this takes the biscuit! And I'm up to my neck in the winter collection.'

Time to crank it up a bit, Jolene. 'I . . . I just don't know what to say, Grandad. Shall I get the next train back and wait at home until she comes back from Benidorm? I've seen this film where this boy does that and he's fine, even when burglars break in to his house . . .'

'No! No—stay where you are—no, listen, do you remember the Italian restaurant up the road we went to last time?'

'I think so. Would it be called Pinocchio's or Piccollino's or something?'

He sighed with relief 'That's it. Go there and wait for me. I'll phone Fredo the manager and tell him to watch out for you until I get there. I'll be a couple of hours at least . . .'

'OK,' I said cheerfully.

'Hell fire!'

Chapter Seven

I had a great afternoon. Fredo remembered me from before because of my Sunderland shirt and we talked football while he prepared the tables for the evening. We were just arguing about whether or not Roma or Sunderland were the best when Grandad Jake arrived. 'Haway, Grandad,' I said, trying not to laugh at his ponytail. He'd have been called all sorts for having his hair like that round us. 'Did you have a good journey?'

He wasn't in a chatty mood, though. After a few words with Fredo, he grabbed my bag and led me out to a waiting taxi, where we sat in silence for twenty minutes until we arrived at his house. Well, I say house. It's more like a mansion. I had forgotten how large it was until the taxi slowed right down to get through the narrow stone pillars of the gateway and entered the long driveway at a slow, respectful pace.

Kirkham Lodge has an orchard and a swimming pool and a stable block and that's just for starters. Grandad Jake is a very rich geezer. Nana must be kicking herself for dumping him all those years ago, though she swears he was a drippy layabout in a tatty duffel coat in those days.

'Now,' Grandad Jake said when he'd switched off all the alarm system and answered his mobile about a thousand times and finally sat down opposite me, 'tell me what's going on.'

 'I told you,' I began, 'Mam's gone on holiday.'

'Yes, I know, I checked,' he said brusquely.

'You checked?'

'I phoned that place she works at.'

'Oh.'

My hands began to shake and I had to press them together to stop them from trembling. The geezer wasn't as green as I thought he'd be.

'They told me she'd gone to Benidorm, yes, but that's as much as I could get out of them. Do you have your grandma's number? She's ex-directory and

BT won't give me it and nor will that stupid salon. "It's not our policy",' he mimicked. Grandad Jake was not a happy chappie. He looked at me, puzzled and sad. 'It doesn't ring true, any of this, Jolene. How would I not know about this? How would Claire not tell me? There weren't any messages from her when I checked. In fact, I haven't heard from her in months.'

'I don't know,' I said in a quiet voice, 'all I know is she's in Benidorm and I'm here.'

Grandad sighed and rubbed his face tiredly. 'Have you got Lynne's number? Much as I hate talking to the woman I need some answers.'

I had to think fast. Believe it or not I'm not a natural born fibber—I prefer to tell it like it is but this was an emergency. I hadn't come this far to blow it now. 'No, I don't know it, honest. I'm not allowed to use the phone, see, not after I called Pluckin' Mel's pretending I was an angry customer whose lips had dropped off because they'd given me too many injections.'

'What?' he said, frowning. I knew what he was thinking. My Brody would never do anything like that; though maybe I was wrong. Was that a tiny smile I saw hovering? But then his shoulders drooped. 'The thing is, hinny, I can't look after you. I'm OK tomorrow but I'm at a shoot in Milan on Wednesday until Thursday and it's no place for kids . . . though I guess I could always ring round here . . . check out babysitters . . .'

'Yes,' I said, trying not to get too excited, 'I don't mind babysitters and it would only be evenings cos I could go to After School club here—the one Brody goes to. It's open from half eight to six. There's a girl there called Alex McCormack who'll look after me.'

'Well,' he said, and I knew he was desperate for any solution, 'I guess we can book you in for tomorrow until we sort something out . . .'

'Yes,' I agreed, 'I think that's what we should do. Sound idea, Grandad.'

'Jolene, just one thing . . .' he said solemnly.

'Yes?'

'Do you think we could drop the "Grandad" tag? Just call me Jake, OK? Grandad sounds so ancient.'

'If you want.'

Flipping heck, I'd call him Homer Simpson if it made him happy. Anything as long as he let me stay.

Chapter Eight

I slept like a log and woke up feeling fantastic—like Sunderland had just hammered Newcastle ten–nil at the Stadium of Light—that fantastic. It wasn't until Grandad—I mean Jake—pulled up outside the school railings on Zetland Avenue all the memories of my last visit came flooding back and I realized my dream of seeing Alex again might turn into a nightmare. Alex would be mint—I knew that from her cool e-mails—it was the rest of them I was bothered about.

OK, confession time. Last time I was here—February half-term—the sparks had flown and I'd lost it with Brody. It was before I'd started having my anger-management sessions, all right? I didn't have a song ready then or anything. Anyway, she'd said something and I'd pushed her down the steps outside the mobile and she'd gone flying. Long story short, she'd broken her front tooth right off and as far as I know she's still having treatment for it. That hadn't been the worst of it. Alex fell out with me for what I'd done and I never saw her again. It wasn't until we got this after-school club 'e-pals' thing going we got in touch, ages later. Then I had to reassure her a hundred times I didn't throw wobblers any more.

But what about me just turning up like this now? I knew for a fact there are at least two people in ZAPS After School club who would gladly use my face as a battering ram. Brody's boyfriend, Reggie Glazzard, for one and her so-called 'minder' Sammie Wesley

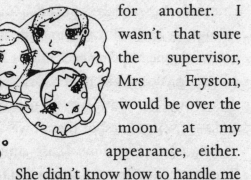

for another. I wasn't that sure the supervisor, Mrs Fryston, would be over the moon at my appearance, either. She didn't know how to handle me like Mick did.

Jake finished yet another business call on his mobile—he might as well have that thing welded to his ear-hole—and began to get out of the car. I was about to tell him I'd changed my mind about this whole thing when I caught sight of Alex in the wing mirror and I was just so chuffed to see her everything else just flew out of my mind.

I leapt out of the car and ran towards her. She was with an older girl I guessed was her sister Caitlin and they both looked startled as this red-and-white striped skinny thing came hurtling towards them. 'Alex, it's me!' I yelled, coming to a halt straight in front of her.

She was smaller than I remembered her, and her hair was fixed in tiny pigtails with flowery bobbles but she was still wearing her top with 'Bad Girl' written on it so I knew she hadn't gone totally girly on me.

'Jolene?' she asked and her mouth opened wide. 'Caitlin, it's Jolene!' she said, her eyes sparkling with excitement.

'Ah, the famous Jolene,' her sister grinned. I liked the look of her. A kind of 'I'll stay in the background but call if you need me' look.

Alex began firing questions and statements like a machine gun. 'What are you doing here? Are you visiting Brody? You never told me! I thought she was away? Your hair's grown really long! How long are you staying, Jolene? Jolene!'

Before I could answer, Jake put his hands on my shoulders and steered me towards the gate. 'Time to catch up later, girls, I've got to see Mrs Fryston.'

'She's not here this week—she's on holiday, with Mr Sharkey. They've gone to the Scilly Isles,' Alex said in a loud whisper, following us through the gate. Blimey, I thought, the whole world's on holiday.

'Who's in charge then?' Jake asked.

'Mum!' Alex said proudly.

'Mum being?'

You could tell Kiersten usually did all this kind of stuff.

'Mrs Ann McCormack,' Alex replied.

'A manic please-don't-let-anything-go-wrong-while-I'm-the-boss-or-I'll-freak Mrs Ann McCormack,' Caitlin added, 'so be good!' And she kissed Alex and left.

No Brody, no Mrs Fryston, no Mr Sharkey. All I needed was no Reggie and no Sammie and I'd be in heaven. No such luck. There they were when we stepped into the mobile, hitting each other with tennis rackets. It could have been my imagination but I'm sure a hush fell as I walked in. It usually does, if you must know. I have that kind of reputation. Sammie looked at me, looked at Reggie, he looked at me, looked at Sammie, wriggled one eyebrow, then shrugged.

Alex linked her arm through mine and made me go and sit with her at the craft table. 'I can't believe you're here. I can't!' she said. 'This is the best!'

'Is it?' I asked.

She beamed at me. 'Is it? Yes a million times a million! How could it not be?'

Relief poured over me like warm rain. Whatever happened when I got found out, no one could take this moment away from me.

Jake spent ages making arrangements with Mrs McCormack. He had to fill out a fresh application form and keep coming over to me to check whether I had any allergies or ailments then go back again. Eventually he was able to leave. 'I've just signed you up for the day. I don't know what we'll do tomorrow—I've got an evening flight from Heathrow booked . . .'

I stood up and gave him a hug, which surprised both of us. 'Well, I've got today, haven't I? I've got today with Alex. That's all that counts.'

Chapter Nine

It wasn't fair—the morning just flew by. There were about a million activities to choose from—outdoor and indoor. I had to admit this After School club was even better than Burnside for facilities. Alex and me spent most of our time on the climbing wall. It was tricky at first, getting used to the footholds and having to climb so high, and Alex wasn't that keen, but the instructors were good at telling us what to do and where to aim for, so we soon had the hang of it. I went up four times and Alex three.

Lunchtime was a bit embarrassing because Jake hadn't thought to pack me any food so I shared with Alex and Mrs McCormack. 'Are you sure?' I said as Mrs McCormack handed me an egg and mayonnaise roll and a banana. 'I can always phone my grandad— he's working from home today.' I fumbled in my bag for Mam's mobile which I still had with me.

Mrs McCormack shook her head. 'Oh, don't bother him. I haven't time to eat anyway,' she said, looking anxiously over my shoulder at Reggie and Lloyd and co. in the far corner who were blowing into empty bags of crisps and bursting them. I had the feeling people were taking advantage of Mrs Fryston not being around. Although there were other adult helpers, Mrs Mac was supposed to be the boss and she isn't exactly the strictest person I've ever met. Still, it was nothing to do with me. I was here for Alex and Alex only.

'Cheers,' I said, peeling the banana.

'Mum, can Jolene sleep over tomorrow?' Alex suddenly asked.

I paused mid-bite, my heart racing. I hadn't even thought of that one.

Mrs McCormack still had her eyes trained on the crisp bag corner. 'What? Sure—I don't see why not—if it's OK with Mr Miller.'

'I'll phone him now!' I cried. 'He said he had to go to Milan so he'd be dead grateful I bet!'

Before she could answer, Mrs McCormack was distracted by other events. 'Oh, Reggie, do you think that's a sensible thing to do with that bag?'

Reggie paused. 'It's just science, Mrs M,' he replied innocently, midway through blowing air into an empty bag of crisps.

'Science?' Mrs McCormack asked.

'Science—you know—an experiment to find out what sort of crisps fly best. Unless you already know the answer?'

'I don't know,' she said, falling right into Reggie's trap.

'Then allow me to demonstrate.'

With one quick movement he clapped his hands together, bursting the bag and splattering shards of crisps all over himself and anyone standing nearby. 'I thought so,' he laughed, picking bits out of Lloyd's hair. 'The answer is plane crisps! Get it—*plane*. Obvious really . . . unless the new Branston Pickle flavour . . .'

'Oh dear,' Mrs McCormack muttered, moving reluctantly towards the lads' corner as Lloyd handed Reggie another bag to experiment with, 'this is what I was afraid of . . .'

Alex linked arms. 'Let's go onto the field—this could turn embarrassing.'

'Yeah,' I said, linking hers back, 'let's.'

While Mrs McCormack had a 'quiet' word with Reggie, we headed for the door. Sammie Wesley was in the cloakroom as we passed, brushing her hair and chatting to another girl I didn't remember from my last visit. As we approached, Sammie swung round and glared at me. 'You'd better keep your hands to yourself while you're here,' she warned me.

Now that wasn't right. I hadn't said a thing to her. 'Or else?' I asked.

'Or you'll see what else,' she said through narrowed eyes.

A few sparks fizzed somewhere in the comer of my brain but I felt

45

Alex's hand squeeze my arm. 'Oh, ignore Sammie—she's in a mood because Brody's not here to hang out with.'

'Am not,' Sammie pouted.

'I don't want any trouble,' I said, 'I just want to relax.'

Sammie turned away and whispered loudly to the other girl, 'Watch her—she's as mad as a brick.'

My breathing quickened and I stared angrily at the back of Sammie's frizzy bonce for a moment. Silently, I began my rhyme for the first time. 'Five currant buns in a baker's shop,' but Alex tugged me away before I could put sugar on top. 'Come on,' she said, 'don't waste time.'

I knew she was right. I hadn't seen her for months and I might only have the rest of this afternoon with her. It was all right inviting me to a sleepover but if Jake somehow managed to get hold of Nana . . .

Quickly, I put that thought right out of my mind. We didn't want to go there, did we? 'Let me phone Grandad before I do anything,' I said, groping for Mam's phone in the bottom of my backpack and pressing his number, carefully ignoring the fact it said there were six new messages waiting to be opened.

My stressed-out under-pressure grandad agreed straight away, just like I knew he would, especially as Thursday was taken care of, too. The sleepover meant an extra day at After School club. Re-sult. 'That's great . . . that's great,' he said. 'Headache over until Friday.'

I was sorry for giving him headaches. Not.

The afternoon was even better than the morning. We got to play football! Real football, with real players from Emleigh Ladies AFC coaching us. I was on a skills team with Alex, a little kid called Brandon, Reggie, and Tasmim somebody, led by this woman called Katie. 'Wow, you're good!' Katie said to me after we had finished doing some dribbling skills through cones.

'Thanks,' I beamed.

'Do you play at school?'

'No—at my after-school club with Mick. I'm going to play for Sunderland Women when I'm older, though.'

'Well, I'm keeping my eye on you, Speedy. We might need you at Emleigh first!'

'Are you keeping your eye on me, too?' Brandon butted in, tugging at Katie's shorts.

'Well, I'm keeping an eye on those trousers of yours,' Katie laughed. 'You must be baking in them!'

I could see what she meant. Brandon was wearing thick jogging bottoms and a heavy, long-sleeved jumper on what must have been one of the hottest days this year. 'I am a bit,' he said, pulling the round collar away from his neck, 'but Mum says I've got to keep them on because of my eczema.'

'Well, if Mum says . . .' Katie smiled and clapped her hands. 'Right then . . . let's have a match!'

Our team took on Sammie and her lot. It was only ten minutes each way and nobody took it too seriously but I loved every second of it. I loved

looking over my shoulder and seeing Alex nearby and I loved watching titchy Brandon surprise everyone by outpacing them and I loved it when Sammie tried to tackle me and I dodged her so, so easily and put the ball into their net by nutmegging Lloyd Fountain, their goalie. Not once. Not twice. Loads of times.

As I glanced across to the side of the field, I saw Katie point me out to another one of her team-mates and say something. And I felt so elated, because I knew it was all good stuff.

From about three o'clock, parents and carers began to pick up their kids. By five, there were only a few of us left. Even Caitlin arrived for Alex. 'Oh,' I said in surprise, 'I thought you went home with your mam.'

'Not now. It keeps things separate,' she replied, glancing at Caitlin.

'Oh,' I said, not sure how I felt about being left alone.

'See you tomorrow, Jolene,' Alex said. 'Bring your jammies!'

'Jammies?' Caitlin asked. 'Are you moving in?'

'Jolene's sleeping over—Mum said she could,' Alex explained.

'There goes my beauty sleep,' Caitlin laughed and tugged at Alex's pigtail. 'Come on—I've got stuff to do.'

They went, leaving me unsure what to do next. Sammie was playing 'Four-in-a-Row' on her own but I didn't fancy joining her so I decided to go and wash some grass stains off my Sunderland shirt in the cloakroom, hiding behind the partition so nobody could see me. I was making a total hash of it and spraying water everywhere when I heard Brandon ask someone if he could take his top off.

'No!' a woman's voice replied sharply. 'I told you to keep it on.'

'But I'm hot.'

'I don't care. You don't want people seeing where you fell, do you? Well, do you?'

'No,' Brandon whispered.

'Come on then—Kagan's fallen asleep at the wrong time as usual— might as well get home before he wakes and yells the place down.'

A tall woman with dark, curly hair swept past, with Brandon hurtling behind her. I watched as she clattered down the mobile steps and threw Brandon's lunch box onto a tray beneath a navy blue pushchair. Not seeming that bothered about waking the sleeping baby inside, she began pushing the buggy so fast, little Brandon almost fell trying to keep up with her. Poor kid. I didn't dwell on it, though—Jake was walking in straight towards me. I needed to concentrate.

Chapter Ten

Talk about tense. The first hour was not too bad—I chatted about what I'd done while Jake microwaved a pizza, but every time the phone rang, I jumped. Was it Nana? Was it Mam? Or even the police? I quickly dismissed the last idea. Nana wouldn't call the police, not so soon. Grandad Martin didn't exactly get on with them and she knew from all the other times I'd legged it I always turned up sooner or later. No, she wouldn't be bothering with them yet. Fingers crossed.

After the pizza and salad I went into the living room and flopped into one of the deep armchairs. I was whacked after all that running about earlier and was tempted to put my feet up on the coffee table in front of me but I daren't. This wasn't quite home.

A minute later, Jake came and sat opposite me, shoved his bare feet onto the table straight away and began tapping his thumb against the edge of his bottle of water. 'Jolene,' he said, his voice very calm but serious, 'I want you to tell me the truth.'

I looked at him and swallowed hard. I'm pathetic at proper lying to someone eyeball-to-eyeball. This was it then. Game over already.

My grandad leaned towards me, his forehead creased. 'You remember last time you came? When Claire brought you here as a punishment while everyone else was supposed to be going to EuroDisney?'

'Yes.'

'But it turned out it was a total crock—they were home all the time?'

'Yes.'

'Has she done the same again? If I were to drive you back to Washington now, would we find her at home varnishing her toenails?'

I felt so relieved I didn't have to fib. I made the sign of the cross against my Sunderland coat of arms and looked him straight in the eye. 'No, she really is in Benidorm, really. Cross my heart.'

Jake shook his head. 'I don't understand it. I don't understand how any mother . . .' He banged on about how irresponsible she was and I began to feel bad. After all, Mam had made proper arrangements for me, it was just I didn't follow them. Then the guy came out with something I had never expected. 'Still, who am I to criticize? I wasn't exactly the best father on earth to her. This is probably her way of getting back at me.'

'Yeah, I think she does wish she had seen more of you,' I said without thinking, but he just nodded in agreement.

'I'm sure she does—I hardly ever saw her when she was growing up.'

'Same as mine—he legged it as soon as he found out Mam was up the duff,' I said matter-of-factly.

'Oh, it wasn't like that,' Grandad protested. 'I tried at first, you know, after the divorce, but my work suddenly took off and then when Lynne met Martin, it became . . . awkward.' He broke off to have a sip of his water, frowning. 'Still, it's no excuse, is it? I should never have stopped visiting. I didn't see her again until she was seventeen. Maybe if I'd kept in touch . . .'

I snuggled down further in the armchair and joined him on the coffee table with my feet up. It was good this, chatting and finding out stuff about Mam. We hadn't had a chance for much one-on-one last time—Brody was always in the way.

'Still, putting you on trains on your own. In this day and age . . .'

Not again! Blimey, for someone who wore a ponytail and trendy clothes who didn't like to be called Grandad he did bang on like an old codger sometimes. 'Jake, I'm fine—I got here, didn't I?'

He glanced briefly at his watch, the same way counsellor-lady does, when the meter's ticking over. I didn't mind. He'd come through for me and that was the main thing. As rich and famous and busy as Jake Miller was, he'd dropped everything and turned up.

As I had guessed, he stood up and apologized. 'Got to make some phone calls, Jolene. Can you look after yourself for a while?'

Who me? Course I could.

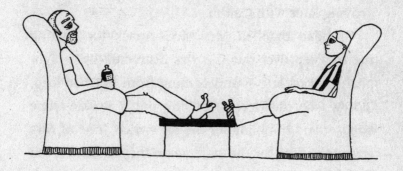

Chapter Eleven

The next morning I arrived at After School club with my backpack all ready for my sleepover at Alex's. I was early because Jake wanted to catch the London train, so only Mrs McCormack and Denise, the student-teacher helper, were there. Alex would be arriving later with Caitlin.

Grandad thanked Mrs McCormack for inviting me to sleep over but she was distracted by a high-pitched crackling sound coming from her handbag. 'Sorry,' she apologized, pulling out a walkie-talkie handset and fumbling for the off switch, 'one of Mrs Fryston's ideas for the staff when they're out on the field.'

'Good idea,' he smiled. 'Anyway, I can't tell you what kind of a hole you've got me out of,' he continued, unfolding his wallet to pay my After School club fees.

'Was Jolene's visit unexpected?' she asked.

'You could say that.'

I looked carefully at Mrs McCormack, to see if I could tell what she was really thinking. I knew she'd been caught on the hop yesterday and hadn't been really listening when Alex invited me. Maybe she wasn't that keen to have me after the Brody thing. I have had problems with friends' mums before—that's the trouble when you're on a short fuse like me: nobody wants their kids to hang out with you. They were always making excuses such as: 'It wasn't convenient', or: 'Maybe another day.' I didn't blame them, either, sometimes! I held my breath and waited.

Luckily Mrs McCormack looked back at me and smiled. 'I wish you'd come more often, Jolene—Alex actually tidied her room last night without being told to and discovered clothes under her bed she'd forgotten she had.'

I grinned. That was OK then.

'So we'll see you . . . ?' she asked Grandad.

'I'm back Thursday so I'll see you at the end of After School club—sixish? I shouldn't be any later.'

'That's fine—I'm here until then. If you're going to be any later, just call and Jolene can come back with us for tea.'

'Thanks, Mrs McCormack!' I said. What a nice lady.

I walked Jake to the door, telling him I could have paid my own fees because Mam had given me the money. I mean, it was meant to be used for stuff like this and there was plenty—there had been two hundred pounds in the envelope when I'd checked. I'd felt a bit upset when I'd seen how much there was. Other grandparents would have done it for nothing.

'It's OK, I think I can manage,' Jake grinned, and bent down to give me a hug. I automatically stiffened, in case he was going to disguise the hug as a hard squeeze that stole the air from your lungs like my other grandad would, and he looked at me strangely. 'You're a prickly one!' he said.

'I'm just not mushy like you lot!' I protested.

Straightening up, he fished in his pocket for his shades. 'See you on Thursday then, Jolene. We'll work out the next stage then.'

'Grandad—I mean Jake,' I blurted, still not really used to calling him by his first name.

'Yes, hinny?'

I took hold of his hand shyly. 'Thanks for everything. I'm dead grateful.'

He looked a bit awkward then. 'I haven't really done anything.'

'You've brought me here,' I said, 'and that's mint.'

'Mint?'

'Mint. The best. Cool.'

He ruffled my hair and looked round the mobile hut. 'Most ten year olds want Disneyland but you're happy with this . . .'

'Everywhere's Disneyland when you're with people you like,' I told him.

'Mm,' he said thoughtfully, 'that could be my new strap line for the winter range . . .' And he whizzed off down the steps, repeating what I'd said.

Chapter Twelve

Like the day before, time went too quickly and all too soon we were having another football match with Katie to finish off the skills session.

I think I was on my fourth goal when Katie blew the whistle and swapped the teams around. 'Just to get a better balance,' she said. It was Brandon, Tasmim, Alex, a couple of eight year olds, and me against Sammie, Lloyd, Reggie, and Sammie's sidekick Sam Riley—every one of them either a Year Five or Six. You should have seen the look on Sammie's face! It made no difference—we still stuffed them. Well, Brandon and I did, if I'm honest. Alex was only playing for my sake—she's not a natural—and Tasmim and the little ones were planks, but nippy little Brandon and me . . .

'Gimme some skin!' I said to him as we returned to the centre spot after yet another goal.

He returned my hi-five and grinned, sweat pouring down his hot face. He was still wearing his thick tracksuit, just like yesterday. 'We're good, aren't we!'

'We're class. You've got some pace on you for a scrap.'

He raised his head high, blinking in the sunlight. 'My daddy's in the army and I make him train me like a proper soldier so I can be strong and fit like him. We play games and combats down the park when he's home.'

'It shows,' I said. 'Is he home now?'

'No, he's in Cyprus for ages 'n' ages.'

'Aw, well, you're mint anyway.'

His eyes shone with pride and I thought for a second that if Jack or Keith had been more like Brandon and liked games, maybe we would get on better. Brandon wiped his forehead with his sleeve. 'Jolene?'

'What?'

'I didn't like you last time you were here cos of what you didded to Brody but I think you're a peach now.'

'A peach! Thanks, bud. Eh, Brandon?'

'Yeah?'

I turned round to see Reggie shrugging his shoulders as he placed the ball in the centre spot and whispered to Brandon, 'Shall we let them have a goal, so they don't cry?'

'OK.'

Unfortunately for them, Katie blew the whistle for the end of the match. 'Warm down first, everyone,' she commanded. 'One lap round the field.'

'Come on,' I said to Alex, 'race you.'

She looked at me and shook her head, blowing hard. 'I can't, my legs are like jelly. I don't know how you do it.'

'It was only ten minutes each way.'

She rolled her eyes at me, still panting. 'No way— see you inside. I need a drink.'

'Me too,' Brandon said, 'a big one.'

'Lightweights!' I shouted after them.

After two circuits of the field and a thumbs up from Katie, I went to look for Alex. I found her in the cloakroom, sitting opposite Brandon and sharing a bottle of water with him. 'Want some?' she said.

I nodded and took a deep gulp. Alex lifted her T-shirt and started wafting it to cool her stomach. 'I'm boiling—I can't wait to get home and take this off.'

'Me too,' Brandon said, rolling the sleeves of his sweatshirt as far as they would go.

'Mate, you're going to faint in that,' I told him.

'Can't you take it off?' Alex asked.

He shook his head miserably.

'Is it because you haven't got anything on under it? I bet Mum's got something in the cupboard you could borrow.'

'It's OK, I've got my army T-shirt on,' he said, and plucked out the hem of a camouflage top beneath his sweatshirt to prove it.

'Take your jumper off then, Brandon,' Alex said and she leaned across to help him.

'No, I mustn't,' he said, pulling his legs up to protect himself.

'Yes you must!' Alex teased, leaping on him

and starting to yank his top over his head; but without warning he kicked her hard with both feet and she stumbled backwards with a yell. 'Watch it, Brandon,' she scowled, 'I was only playing.'

Brandon shrank back against the wall, his face frozen hard.

'Come on, Jolene,' Alex said, 'let's leave him to his mardy.'

Normally, I would have followed her like a shot. Cut that; normally if anyone had kicked Alex like that they'd have been dead meat but instead I shook my head. 'You go,' I said to her, 'I'll be out in a minute.'

'OK,' she shrugged, 'but don't be long—Caitlin'll be here soon.'

'I won't,' I said.

We sat there for a few seconds. 'More water?' I asked, holding out the bottle.

'No thanks,' he sniffed.

'OK.'

A few more seconds passed. I glanced about, making sure no one was around. 'Brandon,' I said in a quiet voice.

'What?'

'How'd you get those bruises on your tummy?'

His eyes immediately darted towards the exit, where parents came to collect everyone. 'Haven't got none,' he said, tugging his sweatshirt top so it stretched like a woollen skirt over his knees.

'I saw them when Alex was messing about. I won't tell, I promise,' I said.

'Haven't got none. It's eczema.'

'Not where you fell?' I said, remembering his mam's reason.

He began to look distressed and I was tempted to leave it. After all, it was none of my business, was it? Only he was only five. And he was ace at football . . . 'See this?' I said, twisting my arm round to show him a scar. 'My grandad did that.'

'Did he?' Brandon asked, his eyes opening wide. 'Was it a naccident because he was tired?'

It had been an accident. Grandad Martin was a grumpy old goat but he had never actually hit me. Threatened to loads of times but never actually done it. I knew plenty of kids who had been slapped around, though. They were the ones who waited outside the office for counsellor-lady with me. I knew the way it worked. I shrugged my shoulders at Brandon and fibbed. 'Nah—no accident—it was from a cigarette to teach me a lesson, but don't tell anyone, will you?' I said. 'You're the only one who knows. Even my mam doesn't know how I got it.'

'No,' he said, 'you mustn't tell, must you, even if it is a naccident or else . . .'

'That's right. Or else . . . ?' I stared at him, as if I'd forgotten what would happen.

'Or else policemen will come and take you away and you never see your mummy and daddy and baby brother again, do you?' he completed.

'That's right,' I agreed, 'that's what they say.'

And he buried his head in his jumper while I stared at my arm.

Chapter Thirteen

'Ready?' Alex grinned an hour later, linking her arm through mine as Caitlin arrived to take us home.

'Ready!' I grinned back and laughed as we did this silly walk together down the mobile steps. Good luck, mate, I thought, as we passed Brandon's dark-eyed, gaunt-faced mam heading towards us.

What do you mean, is that it, you just left him and carried on as normal? What did you expect me to do? Just get lost—go buy a new lip gloss or put some milk out for your kitten or something. Leave me alone.

I had a great time at Alex's house, thank you very much. We played gymnastics on her climbing frame in the garden then came in for tea. Caitlin had made this chicken and orange salad thing followed by double-chocolate trifle and I was allowed two helpings because I was the guest. Her mam had to go out for a meeting somewhere but when her dad came home we played card games like 'Go Fish' and 'Uno' and I laughed because Mr McCormack was a right cheat and he didn't mind who knew it.

Before we went upstairs to bed, Alex kissed this box thing on the mantelpiece. 'What's that?' I said to Mr McCormack as I waited.

'That's our Daniel,' he said quietly, referring to Alex's brother who had died when he was little. 'We still say goodnight to him.'

'God,' I said, 'I never say goodnight to my brothers and they're only in the room next door!'

'That's a shame,' he said quietly.

'You're not kidding,' I said, 'they've ruined my wallpaper.'

'That was one of the best nights I've ever had in my life,' I told Alex later as we snuggled down to sleep. She was on a futon thing on the floor and

I was in her bed, watching the ceiling. Her house is on a main road, so every time a car passes, a beam of light travels across the room. I found it kind of hypnotizing.

'Honest?' she asked.

'Honest,' I said.

'Flipping heck—you're easily pleased,' she laughed. 'Night, Jolene.'

'Night, Alex.'

Even breakfast time felt very different at Alex's house. Although we were doing the same stuff as at home— sitting down, eating toast, getting sandwiches ready for packed lunches—the atmosphere was better. Like when Alex spilt a glass of orange juice across the table, wetting Mr McCormack's newspaper, he didn't yell at her and tell her she was a clumsy idiot, he just laughed and went, 'My horoscope said I was in for a surprise!' and that was that. And when he left for work he gave Mrs McCormack a quick peck on the cheek and said, 'See you tonight, love,' instead of kissing her on the lips for ages and whispering things in her ear that make her giggle like Darryl does to Mam. That drives me potty, that does, and I have to tell them to pack it in, then Mam frowns and tells me to mind my own business and it all starts.

'That was brilliant,' I said to Mrs McCormack afterwards.

She looked at me and blushed for some reason. 'It was just a bit of toast, love. I didn't have time to make anything else. I've got a full house at After School club today so I need to get there a bit earlier. I'd have done eggs and bacon otherwise.'

'It was still brilliant,' I said. 'Thank you very much for having me. I'll just go and pack now.'

Upstairs, Alex teased me as we brushed our teeth. 'That was brilliant,' she mocked.

'It was!'

'Jolene—that toast was as cold as an eskimo's bum and burnt to bits—I'm using my slice for a charcoal drawing.'

'I didn't mean the toast exactly,' I said.

She cocked her head to one side. 'Girl, you're a lot more weird than I remember you,' she said and spat into the sink.

'Thanks,' I said, 'I'll take that as a compliment.'

She wiped her mouth on a dark blue towel and sighed. 'It went dead fast last night.'

'I know.'

'I wish you could have stayed over longer.'

'Me too.'

'Maybe you could next time. For a whole week . . . or even a month!'

'Yeah,' I said, 'maybe.'

The idea was so fantastic, I daren't even think about it too long or I'd ache.

Chapter Fourteen

Mrs McCormack left about half an hour before us and Caitlin walked us to After School club via the newsagent's on the corner for sweets. 'Isn't this mint?' I said after we'd chosen our mix.

'Mint? I thought you'd got liquorice?' Caitlin asked and Alex and I just looked at each other and laughed.

'You two! You're like twins or something!'

I can't tell you how good that made me feel.

The inside of the crowded mobile was already warm by the time Caitlin dropped us off. Sun streamed in through the windows, and Mrs McCormack had to shield her eyes as she reeled off a list of choices for today's indoor and outdoor activities from her clipboard '. . . then for outside, as well as Emleigh Ladies continuing their coaching, Denise is taking Quick Cricket on the far end of the field. It's also the last day of the climbing wall . . .'

'That's us sorted,' I whispered to Alex, 'football.'

Alex looked at me and chewed her lip. 'Jolene? I fancy doing something else today.'

'Like what?'

'I don't know—anything as long as you don't have to move fast—or move at all, even. I might make a macaroni necklace or something.'

'All right,' I said slowly. It was the opposite to what I wanted.

'You can still do football, though,' she said.

'But I want to hang out with you.'

'But we've got tomorrow,' she pointed out.

'Maybe,' I said.

'But we have, haven't we?'

Course, I couldn't say anything to Alex but I wasn't sure how much longer we had together. Gut instinct told me my holiday time was running out. Something was going to happen soon—bound to. 'Macaroni necklace?' I said. 'Sound.'

Alex looked pleased. 'Come on, then,' she said, yanking me up from the carpet, 'before all the places go.'

'Can I come, too?' a little voice piped from behind us.

Neither of us had even noticed Brandon squatting there. Alex sighed and pulled a face. 'I suppose,' she said reluctantly, 'as long as you keep your feet to yourself.'

'Sorry,' Brandon whispered, casting his eyes towards me but I looked the other way. Don't do this, mate, I thought. Don't get attached to me.

'I'll just dump this,' I said, shoving my backpack under Mrs Fryston's desk.

The arty-crafty stuff wasn't too bad, I suppose. I managed to make something that could have passed for a necklace, if you kept it in a dark box and didn't look at it. Alex, though, was in a different league. No stringing orange and green macaroni on a bit of cotton for her—oh no. She was weaving all these delicate red and white threads together on this metal frame thing. It was slow going—by lunchtime she still only had about six centimetres of her pattern completed but I was well impressed.

'What is it?' I kept asking.

'Not telling,' she kept saying.

'They're my favourite colours.'

'No? Really?'

'Yes, really.'

'What a coincidence.'

At lunchtime we all sat outside to eat our sandwiches. We tried to find somewhere apart from everyone else, though Brandon stuck to us like paste to wallpaper. I think Alex was a bit narked but it didn't matter, really. He didn't butt in or anything—he was happy just to sit and listen to Alex and me telling jokes and laughing over nothing. A couple of times I noticed Sammie and a few others glancing across at us but I ignored her, just like I had all week. Not that I'd forgotten what she'd said about me, like. I never forget. I just didn't want any hassle.

'Alex,' I said towards the end of the break.

'Yep.'

'I just want you to know, whatever happens, you're my best friend,' I whispered.

'You're mine, too,' she whispered back, 'forever and ever.'

'Amen,' Brandon added.

Chapter Fifteen

The mobile was stuffier than ever when we returned for the afternoon session despite every door and window being wide open. Mrs McCormack tried to take the register but it was noisy and I could tell she was getting stressed out when nobody would settle. 'Listen carefully, children, please,' she began, 'I have to get this right. There are some new people with us this afternoon and some from the morning session have gone home and I mustn't get them mixed up in case there's a fire.'

She continued droning on about rules and respect and litter on the field, sounding too much like a teacher, which isn't what after-school clubs were about. Nobody was listening. A button on her blouse had come undone and her underskirt dipped below the hem of her dress. Even her clothes disobeyed her, I thought. Normally I'd have got bored and ignored her or shouted out to tell her to wind her neck in but it was Alex's mum, after all. 'OK,' she said finally, 'on to this afternoon . . .'

I had resigned myself to more macaroni stringing when Sammie came up to me just as I was taking my seat. 'Jolene?' she said, a grumpy look on her face.

'Yeah?'

'Katie asked me to fetch you.'

'Why?'

Sammie stuck out her chin. 'She thinks you're a good role model for other girls.'

Me? A role model? That was a first. I glanced across at Alex and she just shrugged and said, 'Go on, role model, what you waiting for? I'll join you when I've finished this.'

'Can I come too?' Brandon asked, scrambling out of his chair and coming to stand next to me.

'Course you can,' Sammie said and she held her hand out for him but he just shook his head because he wanted to go with me and she flounced off in a huff.

'Jolene?' Alex said in a hushed voice as I was about to leave.

'Yes?'

'You'll be OK, won't you? With Sammie?'

'Course I will. It's not like last time.'

Her face flushed pink, as if she was embarrassed to even mention it. 'I knew that,' she said.

I did feel a bit uneasy without Alex at first but my stomach soon filled with bubbles of excitement once the match started. As well as Reggie and Sammie and the other regulars, there were some older kids playing this time, Year Sixes who'd come from another school somewhere. It gave me more of a challenge and I had to work harder for the goals, avoiding some rough sliding tackles from the new kids that had Katie shouting words of warning to them.

One kid in particular, a lanky lad with floppy hair, called Nat, seemed to take it personal when I nutmegged him a few times. 'Someone thinks they're special,' I heard him mutter.

I just laughed and crossed to Brandon. Brandon took it forward but just as he was about to pass back the floppy haired cheat cropped him from behind, taking his legs from right under him. Brandon fell to the parched ground with a thud and started crying.

'Sorry, mate,' the kid said, holding his hands out in surrender as Katie advanced towards him and started giving him an earful.

Brandon was still curled up on the floor, holding his left leg and rocking backwards and forwards.

Sammie got to him first. 'You all right, Brandon?' she said, leaning towards him.

'It hurts,' he sobbed.

'Let's have a look,' she said, reaching for the zip near the ankle of his jogging bottoms to see his legs.

'No,' he screeched, batting her hand away.

'Just to check if it's bleeding or owt,' she said.

'No!' he repeated and his eyes sought mine, like I knew they would.

I had the ball and began bouncing it up and down. 'Leave him alone,' I said to her, 'he's all right.'

She spun round angrily. 'Who asked you? For your information I'm helping him.'

'He doesn't want your help,' I said, coming to stand in front of Brandon but continuing to bounce the ball. Sammie pulled herself up to her full height and glared at me. If looks could kill, I'd have been smoke. A few sparks fizzed in my head and I stared right back. The atmosphere around us grew still and tense.

'Since when have you been the boss of him?' Sammie demanded.

I stopped mid-bounce, and looked at her. Oh, she was up for a fight, this one. I didn't blame her. I knew she still hated me for what I'd done to Brody and maybe if she knew how sorry I was about that she might have cut the attitude, but this wasn't about Brody. This was a different deal altogether. 'I'm not the boss. I'm just telling you to back off,' I said. And I said it quite calmly, for me.

Sammie's mouth almost disappeared into her face and she stepped just that bit too near to me. 'And who are you? The Queen of Sheba?'

I'm sorry, counsellor-lady. I know the rhyme thing's supposed to help but, to tell you the truth, rhymes are rubbish in an emergency. When you've got someone in your face like Sammie was at that moment, those five currant buns just stay in the baker's shop.

I threw the ball to the side and went to smack her one but, amazingly, she got there first and punched me right in the mouth. Though it wasn't a full swing and didn't hurt that much, I was too surprised to punch her back. Nobody had ever swung at me before—they're usually too scared. Besides, Katie was already on the case and pushed us angrily apart. 'Stop it,' she said, 'stop it now!'

'You're dead!' I yelled, darting towards Sammie. 'You are *so* dead!'

'Time out, time out!' Katie barked.

'Don't worry,' I said, glaring at Sammie who didn't have the decency to look me in the eye, 'I'm going.'

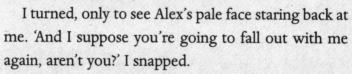

I turned, only to see Alex's pale face staring back at me. 'And I suppose you're going to fall out with me again, aren't you?' I snapped.

She didn't answer but for someone who didn't like sport much she was off like a hare, racing across the field and disappearing into the mobile without a backward glance.

I followed but didn't attempt to catch her because I didn't know what I'd say if I did.

All I knew, when I reached the bottom step outside the mobile and flopped down onto it, was that my stomach had the familiar churned up feeling I always got when I'd messed up again. Brandon came hobbling up a few seconds later and sat right next to me. I slid my arm round his shoulders and we just sat there, like the two outcasts that we were.

Chapter Sixteen

A few seconds later Mrs McCormack poked her head round the door, the walkie-talkie crackling away in her ear. 'No, no, they're here now, sitting on the steps,' she said, looking down at us with a pained expression on her face. 'Thank you, Katie. Yes, I'll wait for her.' Mrs McCormack gave me a disappointed shake of the head.

Here we go, I thought. Same old same old.

I stood up, shrugging as she told me Sammie was on her way over and was very, very upset. 'What a shame, Jolene,' Mrs McCormack began, 'after you'd behaved so beautifully this week.' She glanced over her shoulder into the room where I guessed Alex's sudden arrival had probably tipped her off that she could say goodbye to a relaxing end to the day.

'Sammie biffed Jolene first,' Brandon told her.

'Why don't you go and sit down, Brandon. Katie says you had a nasty knock,' Mrs McCormack replied.

'Not going anywhere,' he said sullenly, folding his arms across his chest.

'Brandon?' Mrs McCormack said, her voice wobbling because he was ignoring her.

'Go on, mate,' I told him and he disappeared inside without another word.

When Sammie arrived I couldn't believe the state she was in. She was blubbering and out of control. What was her problem? I hadn't touched her. 'Calm down, Sammie, please,' Mrs McCormack said nervously, passing the big baby a tissue. 'Tell me what happened.'

Fine, I thought, ask her first. She's a regular, right, and I'm just the bad guy. To be fair, the story Sammie managed to get out in between sobbing everywhere was pretty accurate. She even admitted having a pop at me first. 'So why are you so upset, dear?' Mrs McCormack asked, taking the words right out of my mouth.

'Because . . . because she's . . . she's spoiling After School club for me. I was enjoying coming until she turned up.'

'Sorry,' I said quickly, hoping that would be the end of it.

Fat chance. Once this one started, she gushed like a burst water-main. 'I don't think it's right she's here in the first place—she shouldn't be allowed to come after what she did to Brody. Mrs Fryston would ban her if she was in charge.'

Alex's mam didn't like that much. I could tell. 'Everyone's allowed a second chance, Sammie,' Mrs McCormack said stonily, 'just like you had.'

I didn't get time to wonder what that meant but Sammie turned beetroot. 'Yes, I know,' Sammie admitted, 'but I learned from my mistake. I've never pinched no money again off nobody and I never will!' She turned and pointed at me. 'But *she's* always going to be in fights because that's the way she is! She likes hurting people. The only thing she's a role model for is bullies.'

'As if!' I said hotly.

The tears were drying up now but she was still so full of it. 'Then how come we're stood in exactly the same spot as last time, when you hurt Brody, for just about the same reason? And how come your best friend's disappeared again, just like last time, for just about the same reason?'

And I couldn't say a thing because she was right.

Chapter Seventeen

When I entered the mobile it was like one of those scenes in a school drama lesson where everyone takes up posed positions you just know are fake. Alex was reading a book upside down, Brandon was drinking from an empty beaker and a group of kids were playing Jenga without touching any of the pieces. They were all waiting to see what the nasty girl would do next. Well, the nasty girl was too tired to do anything—sorry to disappoint you all.

'I'm going to just sit and wait for Grandad,' I mumbled to Mrs McCormack.

'I think that's a good idea,' she said, sounding relieved.

'Don't worry, Mrs McCormack,' I told her, 'you'll soon be rid of me.'

'It's not that, Jolene,' she began but I was already in
the furthest corner of the book area I could find.

The rest of the afternoon passed slower than the
last match of the season, when you've already been
relegated and there's nothing to play for, but I stuck it
out without budging. I just sat with my arms round
my backpack and waited for Grandad Jake to arrive. I
kind of guessed Alex would come across but when
she did I felt all tongue-tied and couldn't look at her.
'Jolene,' she said quietly, 'I'm going now.'

'OK,' I said, not turning round. I was in what
counsellor-lady called 'defensive mode' where I put
up a barrier to protect myself. Even I couldn't figure

out why I wanted to protect myself from Alex but I did. Next time I glanced up, she was gone.

So that was that, then. I was Billy No-Mates again.

At last the time came we had all been waiting for. Grandad Jake arrived, earlier than expected and not looking exactly delighted with the world either, to take me away from ZAPS After School club forever. I knew there was no way I was coming back here again. Sammie was spot-on: I'd ruined it. For her, for me, for everyone. 'Ready, Jolene?' he said.

I looked up. Mrs McCormack was hovering behind him—she'd have given him the good news about my behaviour, bet you.

I headed straight for the exit, not looking right nor left, up or down. I strode straight through the playground and into the parking area where Grandad's flashy car was waiting to take me away. 'Home, Jake,' I said, giving it a false smile when he finally caught up with me.

Like Queen what's-her-face, he was not amused. He pointed his key to the car and unlocked the doors. 'Not quite, Jolene. You've got a bit of explaining to do first,' he said, chucking my backpack into the boot.

Great, I thought, just what I needed.

Chapter Eighteen

'So what did she say?' I asked as soon as he started the car engine.

'Who?'

'Mrs McCormack—I suppose she told you about the fight?'

'Fight? Hell's bells, Jolene, you haven't been in a fight as well?'

'As well as what?'

'Here—listen to this,' he said and laid his mobile on my lap. 'Press star.'

I listened, my heart sinking fast as Nana's high-pitched voice screeched on and on and on. 'So then when she hadn't turned up by night-time, I phoned our

Claire at the hotel—I'd been trying her mobile all day but she said she'd lost it—had it pinched at the airport, she reckoned. Anyway, you can imagine the state she was in when I told her Jolene hadn't turned up. "Try that no-mark Spencer at the station," she said, "that's where she always goes first," but of course he'd finished work by then and we couldn't get hold of him till Tuesday morning . . . blah-blah-blah.'

'Press again,' Grandad said when Nana finally finished.

This time it was Mam, more or less continuing the story. 'So he said she'd mentioned Wakefield and so I presume she's headed straight to you so I'd appreciate a call if you're not *too* busy . . .'

'Nice messages to receive in the middle of Milan,' Grandad said.

'Yep.'

'Why did you do it?' Grandad asked.

'What?'

'What? What do you mean, "what"? Run away like that!'

I shrugged. 'I just wanted a holiday.'

'A holiday?'

'Yes—a holiday—you know, one of those things with buckets and ice creams.'

'So you came to Wakefield?'

'Why not? It's as good a place as any, though that walk to the beach is a killer.'

He looked at me sternly. 'Jolene, this isn't a joke. You can't just take yourself off on a whim! You are ten years old! And think how I feel—here's me yelling at Claire when all the time I should have been yelling at you!'

'Well, you'll have to join the queue then, won't you?' I shouted and burst into tears.

I don't know who was more shocked, me or my grandad. Once I started, I couldn't stop. I was miles worse than Sammie. Never mind a main bursting—I could have filled a valley twice the size of Lake Windermere with my waterworks.

On and on I sobbed, blindly ripping tissue after  tissue out of the box that Jake had handed to me. 'Jolene, hinny,' he kept saying, 'I'm sorry. I won't yell at you, I promise. It was just a figure of speech. It's not my style.'

'It's not that!' I managed to sob eventually. 'I'm just tired.'

'Tired? Didn't you sleep well?'

'Not that kind of tired! I mean tired of always being in trouble and tired of everybody hating me and tired of losing friends like I just did over there. Every time something's going all right, right, something rubbish happens and I'm fed up of it. It wasn't even my fault this time. I knew I wouldn't have long before Nana caught me and I wanted every minute to be magic with Alex because she's my best friend and I never get to see her. And I behaved, I did, honest. Katie said I was a role model.'

'So what happened?'

'Nothing!'

'Well, clearly something must have. You said there was a fight?'

'Sort of. It wasn't what I'd call a proper fight but it was bad enough. That Sammie sticking her nose in . . .'

'Listen, Jolene, if something happened at After School club, perhaps we need to go back inside and clear it up now.'

'I'm not going back in there!' I sniffed.

'Well, the thing is, you are. I've booked you in for tomorrow again.'

'I'm not going. You can't make me.'

Jake rubbed the back of his neck. You could tell he was new at all this. 'Whatever happened can't have been that bad,' he began in this corny 'let's-all-calm-down-guys' tone. 'Don't you think it's best to face up to things instead of running away all the time?'

I wiped my eyes clear with the back of my hand, annoyed now. What was the point of telling him anything? He only understood about dumb things like airhead models and orange snowmen. Besides, he had no room to talk, did he? 'Well, everybody else runs away, why can't I?' I told him.

'What do you mean?'

'You ran away and left my mam when she was little and Mam ran away and left me when I was little. I'm only keeping up the family tradition, aren't I?'

'It wasn't like that,' Jake began but I wasn't going to listen to him.

'. . . and you like Brody better than Mam, even though they're both your daughters, just like Mam likes Keith and Jack best instead of me. And don't pretend you don't because you know you do!'

The sparks were coming now, fast and furious. I twisted away from him, pressing myself up against the door as he started the car engine. And then I saw her. Mrs Petty, Brandon's mam, coming to fetch him from the club. This was all her fault. I'd still have that happy feeling and be mates with Alex if it wasn't for her. I wouldn't be leaving here like this, all messed up. 'Wind down the window, Jake,' I grunted.

'There's air conditioning . . .'

'Please!'

He pressed the button and the glass slowly slid downwards just as Brandon's mam drew level with his car. I leaned my head out and hissed at her, 'I'm on to you, lady.'

She turned, startled, just as Jake began pulling away from the kerb. 'Yes,' I said, jabbing my finger, 'I know what you do to him.' Her hand flew to her mouth and I withdrew, my heart hammering in my chest.

'Now what was that about?' Grandad barked, stalling the engine.

'Nothing!' I barked back.

He stared in disbelief as Mrs Petty quickly disappeared into the school playground. 'I don't believe you sometimes, Jolene.'

'Ask me if I'm bothered,' I said, without much conviction, as he glanced in his rear mirror, as if trying to decide whether to get out and follow Mrs Petty or just go home. I heard him swear under his breath and start the engine. Inside my head, the sparks died out, one at a time, and left me feeling totally, totally empty.

Chapter Nineteen

Brody's dad—I had decided that's who he was from now on—drove home in silence, which was fine by me. As soon as we entered the hallway I tried to go up to my room. I just wanted to be by myself. I didn't have sparks in my head but it was full of something just as confusing. I couldn't describe it, but if I drew it, it would be a mass of black squiggles like a cartoon raincloud. All I could figure out was I wanted to be alone, but when I made for the stairs, Brody's dad put a hand on my shoulder to hold me back.

'Jolene,' he said quietly.

'What?' I muttered.

'You're right.'

'About what.'

'About the running away and the favouritism. You're absolutely right and I'm sorry.'

I looked at him and was about to shrug when I got the shock of my life. He had tears in his eyes now. He was as big a wuss as Darryl!

'Don't worry about it,' I said. I felt really confused. My feelings towards him changed all the time.

He cleared his throat and gave me a feeble smile. 'Listen, hinny, I've got something I want to do. How about giving me half an hour and I'll call you down, hey?'

'Fine.'

'Why don't you have a long, cool bath?' he suggested.

Baths are not my thing but I couldn't think of anything else to do so I did as I was told. I felt a lot better after, especially when I dried myself in one of their gigantic white fluffy towels. Trouble was after I only had my Sunderland kit to put back on and that was well grubby so I put on the only other clothes I'd brought with me—my pyjamas—and went downstairs.

'What happens next then?' I said to Grandad Jake, which is what I had decided to start calling him again. It was the name with which I felt most comfortable.

He was sitting on the sofa and had, thank goodness, packed in with the tears-lark.

'First things first,' Grandad Jake said and passed me the phone. 'Claire's waiting to talk to you—just press star.'

'Do I have to? She knows I'm safe.'

'Yes, you do. Don't worry, she won't have a go at you—I've already had a long talk to her. I'll be in the kitchen if you need me.'

I stared at the handset for ages. The last thing I felt like was an ear-bashing live from Benidorm. Mam *not* have a go at me? Who was he kidding? Reluctantly, I pressed 'star' and waited.

The phone had hardly rung once when Mam answered. 'Jolene, is that you?' Her voice came across all muffled and strange.

'Yes. What's wrong with you? You sound funny. Have you got a cold?'

'No, I'm a bit . . . a bit upset that's all . . . after talking to Dad.'

Not her, too! What was this? National Blubbing Day? 'Go on then,' I sighed, 'get it over with.'

'Oh, Jolene! I do not like those two boys more than you.'

It was not the opening line I'd expected but I was definitely not going to let that whopper pass. 'Give me a break,' I said.

'I don't!' she hissed. 'Hang on a minute . . .' In the background, I heard a door bang shut. 'Darryl's on the verandah. I don't want him to hear. Listen, I don't, they get right on my nerves if you want to know the truth. It's just, I have to make a fuss of them because Darryl does.' She took a deep breath. 'He's such a good dad and I want him . . . I want him to think I'm a better mother to them than Tracie or he won't stay with me.'

That was original, I'll give her that. 'Is that supposed to make *me* feel better?' I asked.

She tutted irritably down the line. 'No! But you don't help much with your attitude, do you? Causing atmospheres all the time and running off. Here's me trying to make a happy family and all you do is spoil everything.'

Now I might have bought that a week ago. I know I'm not the easiest kid to have round the house but I'd seen how Alex's family worked. I had something to compare ours to and I knew which one I preferred. The one where if you made a mistake, like spilling orange juice, it was turned into a joke not a fight.

'Maybe you should talk to me differently and I wouldn't spoil things,' I suggested.

'Oh, really?' she said, all prickly.

'Yes—really. And I think you should know that good mums don't have favourites—especially fake favourites,' I told her quietly. 'Alex's mam treats her kids equally, even the dead ones.'

'Oh, does she? Good for her. Maybe she's a more natural mother than I am, then.'

'What do you mean?'

'I mean, some mothers take to it better than others. I'm not a natural mother. I admit it. Do you know what else I know? I hate even *being* a mother! I've hated it right from when you were born, having to be there twenty-four-seven while this little alien clung to me and cried and cried. How's that for a confession?'

It's a start, I thought. Now, I know a lip gloss type would be in shreds if their mam had just admitted she hated being a mam, but the thing is, I wasn't a bit surprised. Let's face it, Mam was only stating the obvious. It wasn't even personal, in a way.

'So what did you have me for then?' I asked out of curiosity.

Mam blew her nose loudly near the receiver. 'Honestly?'

'Yes.'

'Because I wanted some attention from Dad after Kiersten had her baby.'

'That's daft.'

'Well, I know that now, wise girl! I was jealous, all right? You try competing with a supermodel stepmother who's only five years older than you are.'

I should have known it would come back to Brody's mam. It always does, just like when Grandad Martin starts it always comes back to Grandad Jake. Ever since I can remember, Mam had compared herself to Kiersten Tor, and no matter how many times I told her she was pretty and looked young, she never believed me and would get out a photo of Kiersten taken years ago and say, 'Not that pretty,

though.' She even called me Jolene after some stupid song about a woman that takes another woman's bloke away. It does my head in. Still, at least now it was all fitting together.

'Jolene? You still there?' she sniffed.

'Yes, course I am. I'm just listening and taking it all in.'

'Well, that makes a change.'

Now, see, normally with that sort of put-down, I'd have been hurt and said something nasty back and it'd be the start of a row, but I still had the spilt orange juice memory in my head so I just said calmly, 'Yes, I know, I'm learning fast.' Learning to be long-tempered instead of short-tempered.

'Oh,' Mam replied and you could tell she was surprised because she'd been expecting me to kick off, too.

'Tell me more about when I was little,' I said, 'like why you left me.'

'Not that again.'

'It's important.'

She took a deep breath. 'Oh, I just couldn't cope, especially when you got to two and still wouldn't sleep through the night, so I looked for a way out. I took that job on the cruise ships as a chambermaid.

The pay was lousy but anything was better than being at home.'

'Was I such a bad baby?'

'No! This is about me, not you. You were just normal—then anyway.'

'Thanks.'

'I know I should have stuck it out and I know Mam and Martin aren't the best people in the world to leave a toddler with.'

'Huh.'

'But maybe when I get back we can start fresh, eh? You, me, Darryl, and the lads?' The lads. Poor Jack and Keith. Lumbered with two half-baked mams.

'I'll make a deal,' I said.

'What sort of a deal?'

'You stop dumping me at Nana's and I'll try harder to make your job easier.'

'My job? At Pluckin' Mel's?'

'No, your job at home—being a mam.'

There was a long pause before she spoke again. 'Darryl wanted us to get the next flight back, you know,' she announced.

'Did he?'

'Oh yes—he was well worried about you, even when I told him you were like me, a tough little survivor.'

'Oh.'

'Jolene, are you still there?' Mam prompted. 'I've never known you this quiet.'

'I'm thinking about things,' I replied. 'I'm a role model now—that's what we do.'

'Oh, get you!' she said cheerfully. She'd perked up no end. 'Listen, pet, if you want us to come back early and cut our special holiday short, we will do. Though Jake did say he'd look after you until we got back . . .'

Her voice had that wheedling tone she uses when she says one thing but means another. She might be all bright and breezy now but I thought of the mood she'd be in if I said, 'Yeah, catch the next flight out.' Besides, if Grandad Jake was taking the week off, that was a bonus. Ponytail or not, the guy was beginning to grow on me. 'No, I'm fine—you stay in Benidorm,' I told her.

'If you're sure.'

'I'm sure.'

'Will you phone me tomorrow?'

'If you like.'

'Anytime.'

'OK.'

'Love ya, Jolene.'

And I think she meant it, in her own way.

I hung up. I reckoned that was the longest conversation I'd ever had with my mam without it ending up in an argument. And you know what? I felt really proud of both of us.

'Everything all right?' Jake asked, peeping round the doorway.

'Yes,' I said, holding the phone out for him to take. He shook his head.

'What?' I asked.

'One more call.'

'Who?'

'You know who.'

I pulled a face. 'Why? They don't care.'

'Dial,' he said, and went out again.

Like Mam, Nana answered immediately but her conversation was way more predictable. She ranted on and on about me not turning up and what a worry I was and how I'd put them all in an early grave.

'Go have a drink of your special pop, Nana,' I told her in the end just so she'd put a sock in it.

'Your grandad wants a word first,' she said gruffly and handed me across.

I took a deep breath and waited for him to start. 'I suppose you've spent all that money,' he began and I couldn't help it—I just laughed out loud.

'I knew that's all you'd be worried about.'

'Is it?' he snapped. 'How come I spent two nights searching Barlow's Wood for you, then?'

'Did you?' I said in surprise. Barlow's Wood was well spooky—you wouldn't catch me there in broad daylight, never mind night-time. Even muggers avoid Barlow's Wood. 'Oh,' I said shortly, 'thanks.'

He mumbled something about me wanting a good hiding then hung up. I smiled into the receiver. There was another turn-up for the books—Martin Nevin actually doing something that showed he cared about me. Blimey.

Chapter Twenty

This time when Jake entered the room he was carrying a huge glass sundae dish full of different flavoured ice creams topped with fudge sauce and chocolate flakes.

'Waoh!' I gasped. 'Is that all for me?'

'Well, you are on holiday—what's a holiday without ice cream, eh?' he said, sliding the dish towards me. Yep, this guy was definitely growing on me.

'Wow,' I said, aiming straight for the vanilla, feeling very hungry all of a sudden. 'Jake?'

'Aha?'

'Can I start calling you Grandad again? It feels better.'

He smiled. 'Course you can, hinny. It's what I am, after all.'

'Exactly. You've got to do what feels proper, haven't you?'

'You do.'

'Grandad Jake?'

'Aha?'

'What did you say to my mam on the phone to make her cry?'

'I told her what I should have told her when she was your age.'

'What's that?'

'That her daddy loves her.'

'Urgh! That is so cheesy.'

He blushed. 'Cheesy? Maybe but . . . it just felt . . . proper.'

'I think you did the right thing. I think it will stop a lot of problems.'

'Really?' he said and waited for me to explain but I didn't elaborate.

The thing is, when I thought about it, Grandad Jake had caused a lot of problems. If he hadn't become so famous, Grandad Martin would never have been so bitter towards him, and if Jake had kept in touch with Mam, she wouldn't have been so insecure and jealous of Kiersten. You never know, she might even have liked being a mam more. But then it wasn't all Jake's fault, because Nana told me she booted him out, not the other way round, so really it was her fault . . .

I broke off from my thoughts and started in on the pink ice cream. It was delicious. I remembered what counsellor-lady says when I tell her the latest scrape I'd been in hadn't been my fault. 'I'm not blaming you, Jolene, I'm trying to understand.' She was right. In the end no single person was to blame for the mess-up in our family. The thing was just to not make it worse. 'Mam said you'd taken next week off?' I said to Grandad Jake to change the subject.

'That's right.'

'Cool.'

'I need you out of my hair for one more day, though, hinny. Calls to make, models to book—you know.'

'Yeah—whatever. I'll just go for a swim or something.'

'Er . . . not possible, Jolene. I need to do lunch with some clients.'

'So I have to buzz off?' I asked, finishing off the strawberry and starting in on the green ice cream that was turning slushy.

'Yep.'

'You mean After School club, don't you?'

'I do mean After School club.'

'Have I got a choice?'

'No.'

'OK,' I sighed, thinking how thrilled everyone would be to see me turning up again. I couldn't quite see Sammie putting the flags out.

'Hey,' Grandad said, tapping me on the knee, 'just remember it hurts less if you take the plaster off in one quick go.'

'Oh yeah?' I replied, wrinkling my nose at the unexpected taste of the melted dollop of pale green ice cream.

'What's the matter? Is it too tart?'

'No,' I laughed, 'it's mint!'

Chapter Twenty-One

'Ready?' Grandad said the next morning as he parked on the yellow zigzag lines outside Zetland Avenue Primary.

'Yep,' I said, breathing deeply as Reggie and Lloyd went past, eyeing me suspiciously.

'Want me to come in with you?'

'No.'

Grandad handed me a brown bag and grinned. 'Packed lunch. Mrs McCormack mentioned it.'

I managed a smile, even though I had butterflies, moths, and bluebottles flying round my stomach. I think there might have been a couple of bats in there as well. And a parrot. I felt as sick as one anyway but I didn't want to worry Grandad Jake. 'You're getting good at this,' I told him.

'I am, aren't I? Good luck, hinny,' he said, ignoring the ringing tone on his mobile, 'you'll be fine. Remember—one quick go.'

'Thanks,' I said, sliding out of the car and closing the door behind me.

One quick go sounded like a good plan to me. I walked fast, across the playground, straight up the steps of the mobile hut and straight up to Mrs McCormack, who was wheeling the tuck shop into place. 'Mrs McCormack,' I said, 'I just wanted to say I'm sorry about yesterday. I promise nothing like that will happen again. When I think of you, I'll always think of orange juice.'

She blinked a few times, clearly not having a clue what I was talking about, brushed her grey fringe out of her eyes and smiled. 'Well, that's very mature of you to tell me, Jolene. Thank you.'

'That's OK,' I replied, glancing round. I knew Alex wouldn't be arriving until about nine with Caitlin so I scanned the room for Brandon. I couldn't see him anywhere. 'Is Brandon around, Mrs McCormack?' I asked.

She began loading tubs of sweets onto the tuck shop counter. 'No, he's not coming in today. He's not well.'

'Oh,' I said, my mind racing, 'what's wrong with him?'

'I'm not sure, love. His mum didn't say.'

'Is he often away?' I asked.

'No, no he's not. It's unusual.'

'Oh,' I said, trudging slowly to the book corner to have a think. This didn't feel good—this didn't feel good at all.

I waited anxiously for Alex to arrive, pouncing on her nearly as soon as Caitlin had waved goodbye and she entered the cloakroom. 'Alex!' I whispered, pulling her into one of the girls' cubicles.

'Oh, so you're talking to me, are you?' she said as I bolted the door behind us.

It was a bit of a squash but I didn't have time to worry about that. 'Course I'm talking to you— you're my most favourite person in the world—but I haven't time to go into all the making-friends-again stuff. Look, I want to explain about yesterday.'

She flicked a pigtail out of the way. 'No need—I saw what happened. I wasn't cross with you, you know—you just jumped to conclusions.'

'All right, all right, I'm an idiot, I know.'

'Well, now that that's sorted, can we go find somewhere more comfortable to talk than in here?'

'In a minute, I want to explain why I went into a radgy first.'

'Go on then, surprise me,' she said and folded her arms across her chest.

Oh, I surprised her all right. Her eyes opened wider and wider as I told her about Brandon and his bruises and why I'd argued with Sammie and what I had said to his mam outside the gates. 'And he's not here today and I think I've dropped him in it,' I finished lamely.

'Poor Brandon. That's horrible.'

'Do you know where he lives?'

'Why?'

'I thought, if it's not far, I could go round and peer in the windows or something.'

She chewed her lip and looked doubtful. 'That's a bit dodgy, isn't it? I think we should just tell Mum . . .'

'I do, too,' Sammie said from the other side of the partition. This was followed immediately by the sound of a toilet flushing and then a banging on the door. I had no choice but to open it and face her.

'This is a secret, right?' I hissed at her.

'Chill out, Jolene—I'm on your side.'

'What, even after yesterday?'

'Yes,' she nodded.

'Why?'

Sammie began tucking her T-shirt into her jeans. 'Because I believe you. I knew there was something funny going on this week. That daft tracksuit . . . it makes sense now, when you think about it. He usually wears shorts and those army T-shirts, even when it's freezing.'

'I believe you, too,' Alex added. 'Brandon wouldn't have followed you round like that if he didn't trust you.'

'Thanks,' I said, 'thanks for believing me—especially you, Sammie. I know you can't stand my guts.'

'Your guts are all right—it's your face I have problems with!' she grinned.

And I grinned, too, for a split second, before remembering what this was all about. 'Anyway,' I said, 'about Brandon. We've got to keep this between us three, right?'

'No way,' Sammie said urgently, 'you've got to tell. I saw this thing on *Trisha* once—you know, the chat show—and she said the worst thing you can do is keep things like this secret.'

'I'll get Mum,' Alex said and slipped past us.

Mrs McCormack appeared in the cramped cloakroom, a puzzled look on her face as Alex closed the door and said, 'Go on, Jolene.'

I hesitated for a second. This went totally against the way I'd always done things. You put up and shut up. You kept adults out of it because they never believed you and anyway it only led to bigger trouble. And besides, this was Mrs McCormack—Mrs McCormack, who couldn't keep Reggie from blowing up bags of crisps never mind deal with something as major as this. What if she made things worse? 'Tell her, Jolene,' Alex urged, 'tell Mum.'

That's what persuaded me. I wasn't telling Mrs McCormack, the soft teacher type, I was telling Mrs McCormack the mum, who shared her sandwiches and gave people second chances and knew what it was like to lose a little boy. So I repeated everything I knew and watched as Mrs McCormack's already pale face turned paler and paler. I waited for her to tell me she didn't believe me but she didn't do that. I waited for her to go into a panic and say she couldn't possibly do anything until Mrs Fryston returned but she didn't do that, either. 'Are you very, very sure, Jolene?' she asked me and I told her I was and she nodded.

'OK,' she said, 'all back in the mobile now. I'll take it from here.'

A few minutes later she called everyone together, as usual, and went over the morning's choices. 'Now, listen, everybody, I've got to pop out for a while—Denise is in charge until I get back and Mrs Riley and Mrs Fountain are also on hand if you need anything.'

Nobody fussed or asked her where she was going. Only the three of us knew and I'm telling you, it was a long, long morning. There was no sign of her by lunchtime or when Katie turned up to take football.

'No fighting today, you two, all right?' she joked.

Sammie and me both looked at her miserably. 'We won't—we're friends now,' Sammie said dully.

'Yeah,' I said, equally as dully, 'we are.'

'Blimey, what a pair of miseries. Where's that little ray of sunshine Brandon to cheer us up?'

We didn't find the answer to that until we had finished the match. Mrs McCormack arrived back at After School club about three o'clock but of course nobody could ask her anything until nearer home time, when it was a bit quieter. She called the three of us over to the book corner where she could talk in private but all she said she could tell us was that they were all OK. 'Everything else has to remain confidential, I'm afraid,' she explained but added, 'You did the right thing, Jolene.'

'Told you,' Sammie nodded, wandering off to help pack the tuck shop away.

Alex sat with me in the book corner. 'You're not happy, are you?' she said.

'No,' I whispered.

She sighed. 'You know how Caitlin brings me to ZAPS now?'

'Yes,' I said, wondering what that had to do with anything.

'That's because I was reading stuff I shouldn't have been—files and things about it. After that, Mum and Mrs Fryston thought it would be better if I was treated more like everyone else—you know, started at the same time, finished at the same time, kept my nose out of private papers.'

'Oh.'

'So I don't go into Mum's things any more.'

'Course not.'

'I promised.'

'OK.' I still didn't know what she was getting at until she leaned over and cupped her hand to my ear.

'I never promised not to listen to phone calls, though. I'll call you as soon as I know what's happened.'

That girl! She was such a bad influence on me.

Chapter Twenty-Two

The call came just after breakfast the next morning. 'It's for you,' Grandad said, looking surprised.

'Thank you!' I said, almost snatching the phone from him. 'I'll take this in my study, if you don't mind,' I said, marching into the hallway. There, I sat on the bottom step and listened.

'Jolene?' Alex whispered.

'Yeah. What have you got?'

'Everything! Mum's been calling every blooming support group and helpline and agency she knows. Our phone bill's going to be on *Record Breakers*.'

'And? Tell me about Brandon!'

'Oh, right, OK . . .'

This is what Alex Superspy found out. When Mrs McCormack went round to Brandon's house, she found his mam huddled on the sofa with him, staring into space. The baby was crying in the pram and the whole house was a tip. It was obvious she wasn't coping and hadn't been for a long time. Apparently Mrs Petty's mum used to help but she went back to live in Ireland, and Mrs Petty was a quiet woman who kept herself to herself, so there hadn't been anyone else to turn to.

When Alex's mum asked her if what I'd said about Brandon was true, she nodded and burst into tears. She said she never meant to, she just was so tired and stressed she took it out on him, but she swore she never hurt the baby. She told Mrs Mac that what I'd shouted at her had terrified her, in case social services took the kids away, so she didn't dare go out. 'I love them so much,' she kept saying. I began to feel a *bit* sorry for her when Alex told me that.

Anyway, Mrs McCormack has been in touch with all these different people who are going to go round and work things out. The best news Alex overheard her mam telling Mrs Fryston, who only got back first thing and must have been well miffed to be greeted with all this, was the army was going to let Brandon's dad come home on compassionate leave as soon as possible.

'Brandon'll like that,' I said.

'I know,' Alex whispered, 'and Brandon's coming back to After School club next week. Caitlin's picking him up and babysitting for Kagan during the day so Mrs Petty can get some counselling. Oh, Jolene— can't talk. Mum's coming up—gotta go. See you Monday.'

'Yeah, see you Monday.'

'See who Monday?' Grandad Jake asked, looking down at me.

'Oh!' I said, jumping because I hadn't seen him. 'Alex—at After School club.'

Grandad came and sat beside me on the step and handed me some leaflets. 'But, hinny, I've taken the week off. Look, I've just printed these off the Internet. I thought we could go somewhere nice. Devon or Cornwall—France maybe. We could even go to Kiersten and Brody in the States.'

I glanced at the colourful pictures of sunny skies and golden sandy beaches, then shook my head. 'Nah, you're all right—save your money. I'd rather stay here.'

'But wouldn't you rather go somewhere more exciting—somewhere with a bit more of a holiday atmosphere?'

'Nah,' I said, 'but thanks, like.'

He stared sadly at the leaflets. 'Well, what am I supposed to do while you're at After School club? Twiddle my thumbs?'

I grinned. 'Grandad Jake, I know exactly what you can do!'

Chapter Twenty-Three

The second week of my holiday was miles better than the first. It was bound to be, wasn't it? I'd got my head cleared out of all that emotional stuff that stopped me enjoying myself. I was just like everybody else now—one of the crowd.

I spent every morning doing arty-crafty stuff with Alex and nearly every afternoon playing football with Sammie and Brandon. Sammie admitted one of the reasons she'd been in a mardy with me, apart from the Brody thing, was that I was better at football than her. She had been the best girl until I had turned up and 'taken over'. I didn't know what to do about that—a fact's a fact; but Katie settled it by presenting

Sammie with a trophy for best girl player on the course and me with best overall player.

The weather changed towards the end of the week and it rained a couple of times. That was when things got embarrassing because I let Brandon and Alex dress me up in daft clothes from the dressing-up box. I had a long pink bridesmaid dress on with this dumb flowery hat and—wait for it—lip gloss. It wouldn't have been half so bad if Grandad hadn't been there to catch me on camera. Still, I only had myself to blame for that as I was the one who roped him in to take some holiday 'snaps'. Well, I'd reckoned if I had to stare at ones of Mam and Darryl on the beach and Jack and Keith on wherever they'd been with Tracie it was only right they should see me in my element, too.

Of course, my grandad being Jake Miller meant when he had the films developed they weren't the usual pictures with red eyes and half your head missing and a thumb instead of the thing you had meant to take a picture of in the first place. No way, man. These were smart. He had some football scenes blown into poster size and one group shot outside the mobile made into proper postcards with 'Greetings from Zetland Avenue After School Club' printed across the bottom. Mrs McCormack and Mrs Fryston were really impressed with them, especially as Grandad Jake donated a stack of them to the club to use for promotional purposes.

I liked all the photos he took that week but two were my favourites. One was where Alex and me were giving Brandon a fireman's lift. He was wearing a yellow plastic fireman's helmet and a purple tutu and wellies and he just looked so happy.

The second, which is my favourite favourite, is one of me just with Alex. Grandad took it on the last day during lunchtime. We're just sitting on the grass, back to back, chatting. I've got the friendship bracelet on Alex managed to finish at last. I knew that thing she was doing was for me because it was in red and white, I just couldn't tell from the pattern exactly what it was

Greetings from Zetland Avenue After School Club!

going to be. It's really clever, with the letters J and A woven all the way through it. I'll never take it off, ever.

Anyway, I was twirling that round and round and she was wearing my Sunderland top I'd given her and Jake Miller the famous photographer yelled 'smile' and we both turned round at the same time and did just that. It's a brilliant picture. I have it in a frame on my desk, next to my football trophy. What? No, I'm not in the nuddy on the picture or wearing my pyjamas because I'd given Alex my shirt. Very funny. If you must know, Grandad Jake had forced me into clothes shops on that weekend and bought me all sorts of stuff. I'd told him I could just borrow something of Brody's but he said as the one who had carried her suitcases to the airport he could vouch for the fact she had nothing left in her cupboards.

That was the other thing I did that week—I talked to Brody on the phone a lot. I didn't want her getting jealous of me spending time with her dad like my mam had with Kiersten. Brody's not like that, though—she's a laid-back type who takes everything in her stride. When I apologized to her about the tooth thing, she said, 'Oh, forget it.' The only thing that did seem to be bothering her was missing time with Reggie. I had to report back to her every detail of what he was up to during the day. Even what he had in his sandwiches. Urgh! I'm glad I'm not into boys—as far as I'm concerned, they're only good for one thing: tackling.

Epilogue

'So, Jolene,' counsellor-lady said to me next time I saw her, 'how did you get on during the summer holidays?'

'All right,' I said.

'Did you manage to make that list of targets like I suggested?'

'Nah.'

'Oh, well never mind. Did you manage to keep out of trouble?'

I scratched the back of my head and whistled a little tune, making her smile.

'I see. And what about your temper? Did you need to use your rhyme?'

I rolled my eyes at her. 'Yeah, a couple of times, miss, but I have to tell you, as ideas go, it's a no-brainer. No offence, like, I just thought you should know for in future.'

'Well,' she said, glancing at my folder in front of her, 'something must be working. Your teacher says that you have settled into the new year very well indeed, that you are being co-operative, attentive, and sociable and your after-school club leader says simply that you're a star.'

'I'll agree with all that,' I said.

'Well, I think it's fantastic. You won't be needing me soon at this rate.'

'Thanks.'

'Well, come on, Jolene, tell me what your secret is so I can pass it on to the others waiting outside.'

'Oh, it's simple. You just need a good friend to talk to and people who'll listen and believe you and if the sparks start just think of spilt orange juice and when your daft grandad calls you Billy No-Mates just shove a photo of Alex McCormack in his mush.

'Oh, and if you've got a mam that's not very good at being a mam, don't worry—you're not the only one and it's probably not their fault because they probably weren't shown much love when they were kids so the thing to do is find another role model. You can get them in schools or after-school clubs or they might even be in the same family right under your nose. They might even start off as an enemy called Sammie that turn out to be all right in the end.

'Then, if you have good role models, you can become one. Like I'm a role model to Jack and Keith, right. They can both do keepy-uppies now without crying about it and I've got them supporting Sunderland. You can't give anyone a better gift than that. Oh, and Jack e-mails Brandon at after-school club, so he's got a new friend, and having friends is just the best thing ever.'

Counsellor-lady looked a bit stunned as I stopped to catch my breath. 'Goodness! That must have been some holiday,' she said.

I grinned back and twisted my friendship bracelet. 'It was. Can I go now, please, miss?'

Do You Know a Jolene?

Do you have a friend like Jolene? Perhaps she can lose her cool sometimes but she's OK really. Or maybe someone you know is great at football? Or do you have a funny story about someone's unusual grandad?

If you have a story, send it to the After School Club website and we'll print the best stories and find out who is the biggest Jolene of all!

www.oup.com/uk/children/afterschoolclub

starring Sammie . . .

My life's a mess!

My dad's left home, all my mum cares about is going clubbing, and my sisters are a complete pain in the you-know-where.

As if that's not bad enough, I've just told a big fat lie, and I don't know how I'm going to get out of it. How would you get £100 by Monday?

At least things are normal at the After School Club, well, so far, anyway . . .

 ISBN 0 19 275247 2

starring Brody . . .

My family's so screwed-up!

You'd think my life was hectic enough, what with my modelling, school work, private tuition, and After School Club—but now I've got my niece to stay. I'm trying to be nice to her but it turns out she has some major issues with me—I mean, big time.

I thought taking her to After School Club would help, but it just ain't happening . . .

ISBN 0 19 275248 0

starring Alex . . .

It's just so unfair!

Mum's so busy with all her committees and stuff that she never has time for me. And now everyone's saying I've got an attitude problem—well, thanks a bunch.

I think they must have the wrong girl—I'm just misunderstood, an angel really. But still, I'll show them what they can do with their opinions. If they want attitude, they've got it.

I thought Mum being a helper at After School Club would be great—but even that's turning into a nightmare . . .

ISBN 0 19 275249 9

. . . as the girl who becomes a big fat liar
(but whose pants *don't* catch fire)

Before that, though, I had my first experience of After
School club. I was really excited when the assistant
turned up outside our classroom and felt dead
important when she called my name out, then Sam
Riley's. She was called Mrs McCormack—I knew that
already because her daughter, Alex, is in Year Four
and I had seen her loads of times in the playground. I
followed quietly behind Sam, first across to Mrs
Platini's Year Six class where we picked up Reggie
Glazzard but not Brody Miller and then across the
playground and over to the mobile on the edge of the
playing field.

Sam led the way up the three wooden steps. As we
reached the entrance he stood back and said to me:

'Hope you find that your new home will very quickly bring . . . good luck and happiness to you in simply everything,'

finally adding, 'New Home cards, price band F next to Good Luck and Congratulations.' I rolled my eyes at him to tell him to shut up but he just grinned and pushed open the outer door.

What got me first was how colourful it was inside the mobile. Staring through the dusty windows didn't show you the floor was such a bright green and the walls so bright orange and yellow. It made me blink a few times, I can tell you. The kids who had already arrived had settled quickly. Some were playing board games, some were setting out paints on the craft table and others were just sitting around, chatting. Everything seemed very relaxed. Reggie headed straight for one of the computers.

I couldn't take much more in then because Mrs Fryston was standing by a desk near the inner doorway and Mrs McCormack said she would want to meet me first.

'I'll come with you,' Sam went, 'and act as interpreter.' I felt really grateful when he said that, because he didn't need to—he could have just gone off to his shop.

'Mrs Fryston,' he said grandly to the supervisor, 'can I introduce you to Sam Wesley, a friend of mine. She's on the sponsored silence, so enjoy the peace while you can because normally she never stops talking!'

What a cheek. It was true, though, so I didn't have no right to punch him or nothing. Not that I would anyway, with him being so helpful.

Mrs Fryston looked even nicer close up than she did in assemblies. She had greeny-blue eyes that crinkled kindly at the edges and pretty silver earrings shaped like snail shells. 'I'll just go over your details,' she said, checking through my registration form with me. I had to nod yes or no to her questions. 'Well, Samantha,' she said when she had finished quizzing me about allergies and stuff, 'would you like me to show you round or would you prefer Sam to do it?'

I shook my head vigorously. 'What, you don't want either of us to?' she asked, puzzled.

I shook my head again. 'I don't think she likes being called Samantha,' Sam said. I gave a thumbs up.

Gemma and Sasha always called me Samantha-Panther when they were being sarcastic.

Mrs Fryston paused for a second, looking from me to the other Sam. 'Mm. I've got visions of you both shouting "what?" at me when I call out "Sam" though. How about Sammy?'

I nodded. Sammy would do fine.

'With an ie ending, I think,' Sam added.

I nodded again. This boy knew me well.

'Well, then, welcome to Zaps After School Club, Sammie,' Mrs Fryston grinned, and I felt really warm inside.

'Let me show you the shop first,' Sam said, just about dragging me across the room. 'It's not exactly as I visualize it yet, but I'm getting there.' He guided me towards a wooden market stall with red and white stripy blinds painted down the sides. There was a plastic till and huge tubs full of plastic fruit and vegetables all neatly arranged along the top. 'I'm way behind,' he moaned, scowling at a plastic pineapple which had a caved-in side before he disappeared beneath a curtain at the back of the stall and started getting out more tubs but full of real sweets this time. There were jelly glow-worms and gummi bears and cola bottles and all sorts. My stomach rumbled just looking at them. He added a pile of small white bags, a felt pen, and a margarine tub float to his goods.

Before Sam had a chance to finish his preparations, a little boy with pink yogurt stains on his sweatshirt wandered over and held out a 10p to me. 'Sweets, please,' he said.

I looked at Sam for guidance. He leaned down towards the boy. 'We're not open for business yet, Brandon, but do come back later. You can do me a favour, though. You can tell everyone we've got a new club member. She's called Sammie. Can you remember that, Brandon?'

Brandon stared at me and nodded. The tiny kid shoved out his bottom lip. 'I only want green ones,' he said to me miserably.

'Later,' Sam repeated. 'We have to have a drink and a biscuit first from over there,' he explained to me, pointing to a tray full of brightly coloured plastic beakers near Mrs Fryston's desk, 'and nobody's allowed more than ten pence worth of sweets in one night.'

'My mummy's just had a baby,' Brandon added.

I smiled as if to say 'that's nice' and he walked off.

'He's one of my best customers,' Sam told me. 'He's a full-timer, like me, so I've got to know him really well. I'm a bit worried about him—he's gone very quiet since his new baby brother arrived.' Sam glanced across at Brandon, who had taken a Spot book from a rack and handed it to a boy on a purple sofa. The boy looked about my age but wasn't wearing a ZAPS uniform. 'That's Lloyd Fountain,' Sam said, following my gaze. 'He's another regular, too. He doesn't go to a school—his parents don't believe in it. Has his lessons with them at home then comes here to mix with kids his own age.'

I stared in disbelief at Lloyd Fountain. Fancy not having to go to school. I have never heard of that, have you? I know loads of older kids on the estate who don't go to school because they've been excluded but not any that don't go because their parents actually want them at home. I watched as Lloyd's head of curly hair bent over the book he was sharing with Brandon, and saw

142

how he smiled as he pointed out words to him. At least he can read, I thought. If I had lessons at home I bet I wouldn't even know what a book was until I was fourteen. My mum only ever read the TV guide.

Sam shook a tub of cola bottles. 'They stick,' he explained before continuing. 'The only other full-timers are Brody, who's missing today for some reason, Reggie over there, who always hogs the computer unless it's outdoor activities then he hogs the football, and Alex. Alex's a pain,' Sam hissed, as we stared at her squirting orange paint all over an empty Frosties box. 'She hates coming so she makes as big a nuisance of herself as possible. She gets away with so much stuff just because her mum works here. Gets right up my nose.'

I grinned at Sam's serious face.

'What?' he asked.

Glancing round, I took one of the white sweet bags and the felt pen and scribbled, 'And I talk a lot??!!' across the front of the bag.

'Just filling you in on the details,' Sam huffed. 'I haven't even started on the part-timers yet, or the weekly activities. You need to know what's going on, Sammie; you're one of us now, one of the mob in the mobile.'

You probably think I'm being soft, but this glow spread right across my tummy, as if I had just eaten a bowl of creamy porridge. I *was* one of the mob in the mobile, wasn't I? Official.

I scribbled on the bag again. 'YES I AM!! Thanks, Sam.'

That next hour went *so* fast. Sam told me loads more stuff, like how Brody fancied Reggie but Reggie never took his eyes away from the computer long enough to notice and how next time Mr Sharkey 'dropped in' to see Mrs Fryston I had to watch how pink they both went. Sam said he reckoned they were in love which would be cool because Mrs Fryston's first husband had died and she needed a companion. I never knew Mrs Fryston's husband had died. That made me feel really sorry for her, even though it was years ago and she had two teenage daughters and a golden retriever for company.

Do you know what, I think I found out more about people in my school from Sam Riley in an hour than I had in the five years I had been coming here. I couldn't believe it when Dad turned up and it was five o'clock already. He had a bit of a chat to Mrs Fryston and what was nice was everybody waved and said goodbye when I left. After School club was just the best place ever and Sam Riley had a lot to do with that but don't tell him I told you that because I don't fancy him or nothing. I'm not Brody Miller, remember.

* * *

We caught the bus to Dad's flat and met up with Gemma and Sasha who were already there. They tried teasing words out of me but I still had four hours to go so there was no way I was going to give in to their tricks at this late stage. Not for nothing!

After dinner and an argument about who should get the chair and who should sit squashed up on the bed, because Dad's bed doubled as a sofa, if you know what I mean, we settled down to watch *Children in Need*. At first it was light-hearted and funny but when they showed you short films of where the money was going, we all went a bit quiet. Some of the stories were so sad. One boy called Padraic, who was only my age, had something called arthritis. Usually it is old

people that get it but sometimes you can be born with it, like Padraic. Just walking was agony for him and his finger joints were as big and round as giant marbles.

'That must be horrible to have,' I said. It had gone half-nine so I was allowed to talk again but watching Padraic made me too miserable to celebrate.

'Yeah,' Gemma sniffed gruffly and I looked at her, and she was actually crying, but she gave me a deadeye so I looked away pronto.

'Hey, shall we see how much I collected from work for you?' Dad goes. 'I think we did OK.'

'Yeah,' I said eagerly, 'quick—let's count it now!'

Dad grinned and went to the kitchen unit opposite us to find the collection. My heart leapt as he dropped the box in my lap. For one wild second I thought wouldn't it be great if he had collected so much money he had solved all my problems *and* Padraic's? But I knew as soon as I felt the weight of the box that wouldn't be happening and I was right—it was nowhere near. The warehouse collection came to a crummy eight pounds and seven pence and loads of pesetas. 'Well, I don't know who put those in!' Dad said, holding up the foreign silver coins.

'How much are they worth?' Gemma asked.

'Nothing—Spain has euros now. Never mind, here,' he said, digging into his trouser pocket, 'pocket money time. Don't spend it all at once.'

'Give mine to Pudsey,' Gemma said.

'Mine too,' Sasha added.

'You're not kidding me, are you?' I asked but I knew from their faces I wasn't the only one who felt bad for Padraic.

'Well, if we're being charitable, I'd better add my pocket money, too,' Dad went, and handed me a five-pound note which was the same amount he gave us.

'Can't you do better than that?' Sasha asked.

'No,' Dad smiled, 'I need some for myself. I'm going to the pictures on Sunday.'

'Oooh—hot date, eh, Dad?' Gemma teased.

As if he would. She said such thick things sometimes.

'Er . . . how much will that be you've raised, Sam?' Dad asked quickly.

I mentally added the twenty to the rest in the crisp tube at home. 'Erm . . . about fifty pounds,' I said. There was no point fibbing to him.

'That's fantastic!' Dad said, his eyes all shiny and proud and I thought, any other time, it would have been.

I felt a bit miserable the rest of the night and only got to sleep by imagining I was at After School club chatting to Sam and helping him serve out gummi bears.